The Secret City

Carolyn Swift

THE O'BRIEN PRESS
DUBLIN

This revised and re-edited edition published 1994 by The O'Brien Press Ltd.,
20 Victoria Road, Rathgar, Dublin 6, Ireland.
First published 1991.

British Library Cataloguing-in-publication Data
Swift, Carolyn
Secret City
I. Title
823.914 [J]

ISBN 0-86278-382-8

10   9   8   7   6   5   4   3   2   1

Editing, typesetting, layout: The O'Brien Press Ltd.
Cover illustration: Sheila Kern
Cover separations: Lithoset Ltd., Dublin
Printing: Cox & Wyman Ltd., Reading

CONTENTS

For Hani Ali
because he showed me his Petra

CHAPTER 1

The Hidden Passage

Kevin slumped into the white-painted wooden chair on the wide verandah. He looked around in disgust. No swimming-pool, no tennis court, no pitch-and-putt, not even darts, table-tennis or snooker for wet weather. But then, there probably wasn't going to be any wet weather, to judge by the hard bright sunlight that made the rail of the verandah almost too hot to touch. On any other holiday that would have been great. He could have got great swimming practice in, but what good was fine weather when there was nowhere to swim? If only he were with the others at Trabolgan holiday village! This was the pits.

He could see the Shera Mountains across the valley, huge shapes shimmering in the heat of late afternoon. For a second he felt a flicker of interest. It might be fun to explore them one day. Then his anger rose again – they were not here just for one day, or even for two weeks, as they would have been at Trabolgan. They were here for the summer, and then back to school, with the whole holiday wasted.

It wasn't fair. His mother had promised they could go back to Trabolgan again this year. Joe and Gerry and the gang from school would be going and he should have been there too. But then his mother had got this stupid job in Petra.

'You should be thrilled,' she had said, without a trace of sympathy. 'How many boys of your age get the chance to spend three whole months in the Middle East?'

'But I don't *want* three months in the Middle East,' Kevin had said sulkily. 'I just want to go to Trabolgan with the lads.'

'Where's your sense of adventure?' his mother had asked. 'There'll be camels and Bedouins, just like in *Lawrence of Arabia*. In fact, I notice the guide book says the film *Lawrence of Arabia* was shot at Wadi Rum, not too far from Petra. We might even be able to drive over there one day.'

It all sounded like a major drag.

'How far away is the sea?' he asked.

'From the map it looks as if Aqaba's about twice as far as Wadi Rum,' his mother told him. 'I imagine we'd need to hire a car for the day to get there. Maybe we'll manage it sometime before we come back. I'll have to see how far the funds stretch.'

Kevin scowled. What good was one day? He could get on to the school team next year if he could only get in enough practice, but his mother had knocked that on the head now. Why couldn't he have a mother like Joe and Gerry's mum? She stayed at home and baked lovely scones and swam all the year round. *His* mother had to go to work every day in the National Museum. What a bore. But then Joe and Gerry had a father too. Kevin's had gone and died when he and his sister Nuala were not much more than toddlers.

If his mother had even worked in the Natural History Museum it might have been a bit of an improvement. There were stuffed animals and spooky-looking skeletons there. But the National Museum was just full of old bits of broken plates and combs and beads, mostly things that had been dug up at Wood Quay beside Christ Church Cathedral. Even what his mother called 'treasure' turned out to be holy things, like chalices for serving mass and boxes made to hold saints' bones!

Mind you, they'd had fun one time, when he went with his mother to the Viking Adventure Centre in the crypt of St Audoen's church, before it was open to the public. The exhibition was still being put together, and his mother was there to tell the builders how the

Vikings used to build their houses, and how people would have dressed a thousand years ago. It had been a bit spooky down there, specially when everyone went on their lunch break, and Kevin was beginning to think that maybe his mother's job wasn't quite so boring after all. Then she had spoiled it all by getting this rotten job.

'It's the chance of a lifetime!' she had told Nuala and himself. She was really excited. 'I can hardly believe that I'm going to work on an international team, and in Petra of all places! Better still, it's during the school holidays so you and Nuala will be able to come too.'

Kevin had tried to explain to her that this was out of the question, but she took no notice. In fact, he wasn't even sure she had been listening. She was only thinking about telephoning her boss at the museum, and the travel agents, and all her friends, so she could tell them the great news. And now here they were, in a place called Wadi Musa, in the middle of nowhere, where the Jordanian government had given them a house for the summer.

Kevin could hear his mother's voice from somewhere inside the gleaming white building. He reckoned she was talking to the driver, telling him where the cases were to go. He didn't look at all like the driver of a taxi, Kevin had thought as they drove down the long, dusty desert highway from Amman, more like some kind of prophet, with his loose white robes and the red-and-white check cloth that he wore on his head. It looked like an oversize duster.

Everything except that was white, Kevin noticed: house, chairs, clothes, everything. And even now, though it must be getting late, the sun was still blinding. His eyes ached from its brightness and the heat was making him feel irritable. His T-shirt was drenched with sweat. If it was this hot now, what would it be like at midday? It would be far too hot to play tennis anyway – even if there *was* a tennis court.

'Kevin! Come and see your room!'

His mother's voice came from somewhere above him. Kevin looked up and saw her on a white stone balcony which jutted out from the wall opposite. He heaved himself wearily to his feet and walked through a curtain of hanging, rattling beads into the living-room.

At the other end of the room, Nuala was talking to a slim blond girl in a pale blue dress. She was no taller than Nuala, though his sister's stocky build always made her seem shorter, but the other girl had to be older. She was wearing lipstick and nail varnish, Kevin noticed.

'This is Amanda Houston,' Nuala said. 'She's here with her parents. They've already been here for three days.'

'Hi!' Kevin grunted. 'Is there anything to do around here?'

'Sure!' She was American. That nasal twang in her voice was unmistakable. 'There's horseback riding in the mountains. My dad's hired a pony for me for the summer. She's a beauty, pure Arab. You can come with us if you can keep up.'

Kevin said nothing, but of course Nuala had to open her big mouth.

'We never learned to ride,' she blurted out.

'Gee, I thought everybody in Ireland lived in the saddle,' Amanda exclaimed loudly. 'How d'you get around on the bog if you can't ride?'

'We don't live in a bog,' Kevin snapped, 'and we don't keep coals in the bath or catch leprechauns either!' Americans! he thought, turning his back on the girls.

He climbed up the cool white curving stairs up to a wide landing, and found his mother, pottering about as usual.

'This is your room,' she told him. 'Isn't it nice? You can look right down the hill to the Rest House opposite.'

'What's that stuff on the window?' Kevin asked. Instead of glass, there was netting with tiny holes.

'That's to keep out the mosquitoes,' his mother replied. 'The air gets through but *they* don't. Once the sun goes down you must keep them closed if you don't want to be eaten alive.'

'It's very hot in here,' Kevin complained.

'You must always keep the shutters closed during the day if you want to stop it from getting like an oven,' was all she said in reply.

'Doesn't sound as if it matters *what* I can see from the window,' Kevin grumbled, 'if I've got to keep the shutters closed all day and the netting closed at night.'

'Oh, come on!' his mother cried impatiently. 'You're not going to sulk for the whole three months, are you? Make up your mind to enjoy yourself and you'll have a great time. The dig director's daughter seems happy with everything.'

'I wouldn't mind that stuck-up twit,' Kevin scoffed.

'It's obviously a waste of energy talking to you in the mood you're in at the moment,' his mother told him. 'I've a thousand and one things to see to, so you can get your case unpacked by yourself. You should be able to manage that at least. And then come on downstairs. We're going to have tea at the Rest House this evening. I've enough to do without getting meals right away.'

The Rest House turned out to be a sort of hotel, but Kevin didn't think much of the restaurant. It had stone walls and ceiling, and large rectangular niches were cut all around the room in the same rough shape as the door. It was quite chilly after the heat of the day, and was dimly lit and slightly eerie.

'Looks like a tomb!' Kevin grimaced.

'Very smart of you!' his mother laughed. 'That's exactly what it used to be: the tomb of Al Khan. It's like many of the simpler ones inside Petra.'

'Yuk!' Kevin said. 'Who'd want to eat in a tomb?'

'Most people who come here,' his mother told him, still laughing. 'It's one of the attractions of Wadi Musa. After you've seen Petra maybe you'll understand.'

Kevin thought that was unlikely, as he followed the others inside. There were three long tables in the middle of the room.

'Do they expect us to share with other people?' he asked, for the tables would each have seated twenty or more.

'They're for the package tours,' his mother explained. 'People come down from Amman for the day by coach or on the jet bus, visit Petra, lunch here, and then go back in the afternoon after they've seen the museum.'

Of course, Kevin thought, there *had* to be a museum. They all sat down, Kevin beside his mother, opposite Amanda and her mother, and Nuala between her mother and Amanda's father at the head of the table. Kevin glowered at Amanda, wishing she didn't look so elegant. She had changed out of her blue linen into a warm woollen dress in a soft mossy green, so of course she wasn't feeling the cold.

'It will be nice for you and Nuala to have Amanda here,' his mother had said. 'And she comes right between the two of you in age too.'

Kevin had stared in amazement. How could Amanda, with her lipstick and nail varnish, be younger than himself?

'I thought she must be sixteen at least,' he said.

'She certainly seems to be a very sophisticated young lady,' his mother smiled, 'but her father assures me she's younger than you are. It must be her New York background.'

Kevin looked at the menu that stood up against his glass, but he couldn't make head nor tail of it. There were lines of curls and squiggles with little dots above and below them.

'It's got funny writing on it,' he announced.

'Arabic,' Amanda's mother told him. 'I guess we'll just have to ask the waiter what we can have. Get him over here, Chuck, will you? We don't want to sit here all night.'

Amanda's father called the waiter over and asked what there was to eat.

'Chicken or lammy meat,' the waiter said solemnly.

'Chicken or *what*?' Kevin asked him.

'Lamb,' Amanda's father told him, 'but you can take

it that means mutton. It'll be tough and the chicken's kinda dry, but they're both quite edible.'

'Is that all?' Nuala asked. 'There's rows and rows of squiggles.'

'The rest are starters and dessert,' Amanda told her, 'and I guess they're always the same too. There'll be olives or hummus for starters and baklava or halva for dessert. And afterwards there's that ghastly thick coffee that leaves grounds in your mouth.'

'What did you say there was besides olives?' Kevin asked.

'Hummus,' Amanda repeated. 'I like it a lot. It's made out of chick peas and sesame oil.'

Kevin pulled a face.

'I think I'll just have bread,' he said.

'You're not very adventurous, are you?' his mother commented. 'You should at least try the local food. You might find you loved it.'

'You'll adore the baklava,' Amanda told him. 'I'm only crazy about it.'

'Too sweet for me,' Amanda's mother said, 'and ruinous for my diet, but you kids oughta like it.'

'I'll give it a try,' Kevin grunted, 'and I'll have the chicken, but I don't want any of that stuff that sounds like turf mould.'

'I'll taste some of yours, Mum,' Nuala said, 'and then if I like it I can have it another time.'

'Good girl!' his mother said and Amanda's father nodded.

'Very sensible,' he agreed. 'That's the best way to find out about anything new.'

Trying to impress the Houstons, Kevin thought disgustedly. Just like a girl!

The waiter put a plate down in the centre of the table. On it were what looked like folded pancakes.

'What's that?' Kevin asked.

'You not want?' the waiter asked.

'Yes, that's fine. Thank you,' Kevin's mother said quickly and then, turning to Kevin, added: 'You asked for bread. Now eat it!'

'That's not bread,' Kevin protested.

'There's only two kinds of bread in these parts,' Mrs Houston explained to him. 'This here is pitta bread and the other's kinda thinner and flatter.'

You can't even get decent bread, Kevin thought. What a dump!

The waiter came back with funny little dishes of white stuff that looked a little like porridge. He put one in front of Kevin, but Kevin pushed it away.

'I said I didn't want any,' he pointed out.

His mother ignored him. She was busy spreading a little of her own on a small piece of pitta bread and handing it to Nuala.

'Mm, yummy!' Nuala said the minute she tasted it.

'Have we an early start in the morning?' her mother asked Mr Houston.

'If you're not too tired after driving down today,' he replied. 'It's best to do as much as we can before it gets too hot. By twelve it's impossible. We break then, start again around three and work till the light goes. You'll find it gets dark fast once the sun starts to sink.'

'I noticed that this evening,' Kevin's mother said. 'When I started unpacking it was like midday but, before I was finished, I had to switch on the light.'

'I guess it's something to keep in mind,' Mr Houston told her. 'You wouldn't want to get caught walking through the Siq by yourself after dark.'

'What's the Seek?' Kevin asked.

'The passage through the mountains into the Secret City,' Mr Houston replied. 'They've widened it now but when Burckhardt discovered it in 1812 it was just a narrow cleft in the cliff-face. Nobody would ever find it unless they knew where to look. That's how Petra remained unknown for over a thousand years. Even today the cliffs almost meet overhead in spots. It can be quite frightening there except when it's crowded with tourists.'

'But why can't you go through it after dark?' Kevin asked, thinking it might be fun.

'You're real isolated in there,' Mrs Houston

answered. 'You could scream your head off and nobody'd hear you. With all the twists and turns in it, it's got to be the best part of one-and-a-half kilometres long and the cliffs on either side are over eighteen metres high.'

'Only the Bedouins go there on foot at night,' Mr Houston added.

'I wouldn't object to being carried off by a Bedouin sheik,' Amanda giggled, 'but I'm terrified of the scorpions hiding out in the cracks in the rocks.'

'Scorpions!' Nuala gasped.

'With their tails cocked in the air,' Mrs Houston said, 'and a terrible sting in their tail!'

'And you can forget Amanda's romantic nonsense,' her father added. 'This isn't Hollywood. You wouldn't be carried off, you'd be mugged.'

'And you're not at home in Ireland either,' Mrs Houston said, 'so watch out for snakes. I guess St Patrick never came to Petra to banish them.'

'Are they poisonous?' Nuala asked anxiously.

'They sure are,' Mr Houston said emphatically, 'but you probably won't come across any if you stick to the tracks. They like to curl up in the hollows of the rock where the sun has warmed it, so just watch where you're putting your feet if you go climbing and don't go poking your fingers into any crannies. That oughta take care of both the snakes and the scorpions.'

The place was sounding less attractive every minute, Kevin thought. Anything that wasn't boring seemed to be dangerous.

'Will we be coming back to Wadi Musa at twelve?' his mother was asking.

'Sure. It doesn't take long in the jeep and that way we can get an hour or so of shut-eye. You won't feel like eating much in the heat. A bit of fruit and some cheese maybe. My guess is that you'll be more thirsty than hungry. You'll want to take plenty of fluids or you'll get dehydrated. No alcohol, but plenty of tea, soft drinks or bottled water.'

'And what do *we* do?' asked Kevin.

'Can't you explore Wadi Musa?' his mother answered impatiently.

'I think you oughta let them come with us tomorrow,' Mr Houston said. 'Once they've seen Petra they'll find plenty to do.'

'Won't they be in the way?' his mother asked uneasily – as if they were small children, Kevin thought crossly.

'They don't have to hang around the dig,' Mr Houston told her, 'but they might as well come for the ride so long as we're going. It's a long way to walk. That's why the tourists all go in on horseback. D'you want to come with them, Sue?' He turned to his wife.

Mrs Houston shook her head.

'Amanda and I are gonna take the horses on a trek in the Shera Mountains,' she said. 'I guess I've seen enough of tombs over the past three days.'

It was all being decided for them, Kevin thought in disgust, but at least it meant he wouldn't have to be with that silly, giggly Amanda.

'Okay,' he agreed. 'There doesn't seem to be anything better on offer.'

When his mother banged on his door at seven the next morning, however, all he wanted was another few hours' sleep.

'Please, Mum,' he groaned, squinting up at her with one eye still closed. 'Let me stay here! I'll see you when you get back at twelve.'

Dressed in her working overalls, his mother stood looking down at him. 'I suppose after that long journey in the heat yesterday you were bound to be tired,' she said, sympathetic for once. On a school day she would just have ripped the bedclothes off him, but then there had only been one light cotton sheet on his bed last night and now even that was on the floor. 'Nuala seems dead to the world too,' she continued, 'and I suppose when all's said and done, it is your holiday.'

To Kevin's relief, she went away then but, before he could drop off again, she was back.

'Mrs Houston very kindly said she would leave you and Nuala down to the mounting block when the jet bus arrives at ten,' she told him, 'and you can go through the Siq on horseback with the tour. She and Amanda decided against an early start for their ride, so she'll give you a call at half-nine. You *will* get up right away for her like a good boy, won't you?'

'Yeah, yeah, yeah!' Kevin mumbled, and went back to sleep again. Next thing he knew, Mrs Houston was banging on his door. Reluctantly, he tumbled out of bed. The sun was already blazing down as he pushed back the mosquito netting window and closed the shutters. He still felt tired but he did remember promising not to give Mrs Houston any trouble. Besides, it was already too hot in his room to want to stay in it much longer.

When he got downstairs, Nuala and Mrs Houston were ready and waiting for him. The three of them set off down the hill, past the Rest House and along the valley his mother called the *wadi*. Ahead he could see a crowd of people and horses milling around a large stone. Only then did he remember that his mother had said something about going on horseback. Nuala must have remembered at the same moment.

'I've never ridden before,' she said nervously.

'By the look of the others I'd say most of them gotta be in the same boat,' Mrs Houston laughed. 'I guess these ponies must be well used to folk that were never in the saddle in their lives. You'll have a Bedouin to lead you so there's no call for panic. Just give him this when you get to the Treasury.'

Kevin looked at the coins she held out to him, hesitating.

'It's okay, your mother gave it to me to give you,' she said. 'You'll know when you get to the Treasury because the ponies turn around and come back then. And don't let them tell you it's not enough money. It's plenty!'

They joined the crowd around the mounting block. A lean, dark-skinned man in white robes and head-dress was helping a large lady to climb from the mounting block into the saddle of a sturdy pony, which waited patiently to receive its burden. Even when she clutched at the pony's mane it never stirred and Kevin felt a little relieved. He and Nuala could hardly do much worse.

Mrs Houston spoke to a man with a moustache who held the pony that was next in line. He nodded, motioning Nuala to climb on to the stone. When she managed to clamber unaided from there into the saddle, the man nodded approvingly and put the reins

– a rough rope running from rings at either end of a chain which circled the pony's nose – in her hands.

Then it was Kevin's turn. His pony seemed to be asleep in the heat, and moved only occasionally to flick his ears at the flies buzzing around his closed eyes. Kevin decided that this was just like the vaulting horse in the school gym. He sprang from the stone with such bravado that the pony moved forward a step or two in surprise. Kevin almost slid right over the opposite side of the horse, but he managed to grab the front of the saddle and steady himself. The driver grinned, shoving Kevin's feet into the stirrups. There was a man ahead of him who sat easily in the saddle as if he was well used to horses, so Kevin copied the way he was sitting – knees gripping the pony's flanks, heels pushing down, toes turned outwards.

'These two won't be going on the tour,' Mrs Houston told the man. 'When they get to the Treasury, will you point them towards the archaeological dig?'

The man nodded. Then he pulled on the reins of Kevin's pony with one hand and Nuala's with the other and made a little clucking sound. As soon as they heard it, the ponies turned and walked off down the wadi after the others. They were on their way.

At first Kevin was too busy trying to sit comfortably in the saddle to notice where they were going. Then he saw that they were following a wide, sandy track with low mountains on either side. They were the strangest mountains he had ever seen, softly rounded and covered in weird bumps and lumps. And the cliffs, which had looked continuous from a distance, now looked almost like a row of terraced houses, all different shapes and sizes, with taller terraces sticking up behind. There were lots of openings cut into the cliff face too, some shaped like rough doors and windows, others no more than hollows. Caves, Kevin thought, suddenly interested. He had always liked caves and this place was full of them.

'Look!' Nuala shouted, pointing to the opposite side of the wadi. 'Somebody has cut shapes into the mountainside!'

The whole group looked across to where she was pointing.

'Tomb,' said the man who was leading their ponies.

'But it's a cave!' Kevin exclaimed, for they could see that what looked like a big door into some ancient palace really led straight into the side of the mountain. 'Someone has cut the rocks on either side of the cave to make it look like pillars!'

'And there's another one on top,' Nuala pointed out. This one didn't look at all like a palace though. It was more like a rectangular door cut in the middle of a wall. Around the doorway there were four pillars carved into the cliff face, squared and pointed at the top.

'Tomb of Obelisk,' said the man holding the reins.

Kevin started looking more closely at the mountains after that. He knew now that the reason so many of them looked like houses was because that was exactly what they were, though apparently they were houses intended only for the dead. Suddenly it seemed as if they could go no further. A wall of rock blocked their path, yet the white-robed men still led the horses forward. Then he remembered Mr Houston saying that no-one would ever find the Siq unless they knew it was there. He scanned the rock-face but could see no opening anywhere. Then, where the cliff seemed to hang in folds like curtains, the leading horse suddenly swung in to the left. Only then did Kevin realise there was a space hidden in the folds of rock. As his own pony followed, he saw they were entering a winding passage leading straight into the cliff.

Walls of rock rose on either side of them, shutting out the sun. It was like riding into the twilight. The rock was strangely coloured too, now greenish-blue, now slate-grey and darkening to black in the folds. Tilting his head back as far as he could, Kevin could just see a narrow slit of sky, as far above him as the roof of a cathedral.

The passage was wide enough to drive a jeep

through now, but he could tell from the slit above how narrow it had been before they widened it. It was no wonder Petra had remained hidden for so long.

As they rode deeper and deeper into the heart of the rock, the voices of the riders became more and more hushed. He could hear nothing but the snorting of the small but powerful Arab ponies and the ring of their hooves as they struck off loose stones in the sand underfoot. Even the large lady in front had fallen silent, so that, when a bird flew out from somewhere high up in the cliff with a sudden harsh cry, Kevin started with fright. Now that the heat of the sun was cut off, he could feel a chill through his cotton shirt.

A whole invading army could have been ambushed and wiped out in a place like this, he thought. How many men had died here over the centuries? A bead of cold sweat fell from his forehead on to his bare arm. He knew now why Mr Houston had said they mustn't go through here on their own after dark. It was a place of mystery, intrigue and fear.

CHAPTER TWO

The Hole in the Wall

It felt as if they had been riding through this crack in the mountains for ages, Nuala thought. There were little shrine-like niches to either side, cut into the rock, which was the colour of the sea when the light shone through it. At other times, when the cliffs almost touched overhead and only a crack of light penetrated, the walls were black and shadowy, so that it was like travelling into nowhere.

Suddenly she saw light ahead. It was so brilliant in contrast with the darkness of the Siq that it dazzled her eyes. Then, as they became used to the sun's brightness, she saw a white pillar, lit by the sun as if by the beam of a spotlight.

'Oh,' the woman ahead cried, 'look!'

As she followed her out of the Siq and felt the heat of the sun on her body once more, Nuala cried out too, for straight ahead was a great palace. The six pillars in front of it were so tall that the people standing nearby looked no bigger than ants. Between the middle two pillars, a flight of steps led up to the portico, and from the back of the portico a further flight led up to a massive doorway. Over its decorated pediment were twelve more pillars, the four in the centre holding up a great rounded dome, topped by an urn. In the spaces between the pillars were pedestals supporting the remains of statues, so old that most of their heads were worn away. Then Nuala realised that the whole building was set into the side of the cliff, just as a picture is set into a frame. She realised, too, that the stone wasn't white at all.

'That's funny,' she remarked to Kevin. 'I thought when I first saw the pillars that they were white, like icing sugar, but the whole building's pink.'

'Treasury pink now,' said the man holding her pony. 'Later will be red, then orange. Every hour stone changes colour as sun moves. Later still will be gold. Now you pay me.'

'Right,' said Kevin, sliding awkwardly to the ground. 'This is for the two of us.'

The man looked at the coins, hesitated for a minute, and then decided to accept them.

'Shukran!' he said, putting the coins somewhere inside the folds of his white robes. Then he lifted Nuala down. 'That way to dig,' he said, pointing to their right along the narrow wadi. 'You see men working near great temple of Dhu-Shara.'

Then he mounted the pony Kevin had been riding, turned it and cantered off into the Siq, leading Nuala's pony by the reins. A tall dark man in Bedouin robes, with a nose like a hawk's beak, appeared. He came forward to meet the group, which was standing gazing in awe at the Treasury.

'I guide for you this morning,' he announced. 'My name Hassan. Come with me, please!'

'We don't go with him,' Nuala said, as Kevin started to follow him towards the Treasury.

'I know,' Kevin agreed, 'but we may as well see over this place before we go. It's fantastic!'

'I bet there's nothing to see inside,' Nuala said, as they joined the group around the guide at the foot of the steps. 'It's just a pretend palace, like the one we saw on the way here.'

'This has real pillars,' Kevin argued, 'not like the other one that only has pillar-shapes carved into the rock. The space behind these pillars is as big as a shopping arcade.'

'Ssh!' said the man standing beside Kevin. 'I want to hear the guide.'

'El Khazneh Fara'un, meaning Treasury of Pharaoh,' the guide was saying, 'was given this name because people believe treasure of Pharaohs hidden in great stone urn. For many years they shoot at urn to break it. You see there many bullet holes in front, yes? But cannot break. Of course, people wrong. Is not Egyptian palace but Nabatean tomb.'

Nuala nudged Kevin.

'I told you so,' she whispered.

'Petra was capital city of Nabatean people,' the guide continued. 'Treasury is ninety-two feet wide, one hundred and thirty feet high and more than one thousand five hundred years old. Is cut into sandstone cliff to look like palace because was tomb for king. Treasury is best-preserved building in Petra because cliff hang over, protect Treasury from wind and rain. Sandstone very soft, so only here not badly worn as other tombs.'

He turned to go on down the valley but a man stopped him.

'Can't we go inside?' he asked.

'Is nothing to see,' Hassan shrugged, 'but you want see, I wait.'

Kevin darted ahead of the group up the steps and in through the great carved doorway. Most of the group followed, but Kevin was back out again before they had reached the second flight of steps.

'It's only like a cave inside,' he told Nuala. 'Just one big room, really, with a few hidey-holes off it.'

'I knew it would be like that,' Nuala said. 'Come

on. Let's go.'

'You wait, please,' Hassan called after them as they walked off, 'or you get lost!'

'No, we won't!' Kevin called back. 'We aren't going with you.'

'You come here, please!'

Suddenly he sounded quite fierce, Nuala thought. She felt glad they weren't going with him.

'What is it?' she asked reluctantly.

'You not on my tour?' he asked.

'We just rode in with the others,' she explained. 'We're going to my mother who is on the dig beside the Dhu-Shara Temple.'

'Then you go,' Hassan ordered. 'But remember, this is not playground for children. This ancient city, home of Bedouin people. You stay on path. No climb cliffs. Many rocks fall. You want see tombs you pay guide.'

'Okay,' Nuala said. 'We'll do that.'

Hassan still didn't seem satisfied, though.

'Remember I say this,' he continued. 'You think mother know everything. I, Hassan, say archaeologist know plenty, Bedouin know *more*. Many things in Petra only Bedouin know. Is much danger for foolish one who think he know more than Bedouin.'

'I'll remember,' Nuala said. Then she turned on her heel and hurried on along the sandy track towards the dig.

'He's scary,' she gasped when she caught up with Kevin.

'Oh, don't mind him,' Kevin replied. 'He was only annoyed because we'd heard his party piece without paying for it.'

'But he said we were to stick to the track,' Nuala told him, 'though I can't see why. Look over there, to the left. There are loads of tourists climbing the cliffs.'

'He doesn't want us to look at them without paying a guide,' Kevin said, 'but I think we should go straight to the dig now anyway. Otherwise Mum will wonder what's happened to us. We've three whole months to explore and we're not paying old Hawk-Face every time we want to go into a tomb.'

Nuala couldn't help feeling there was more to Hassan's warning. They could ask Mr Houston if it would be all right to go into the tombs on their own.

As they walked on, they could see dozens of tombs laid out in terraces running up the side of the mountain. These were not like palaces with great pillars and statues, though. They were more like houses, really. They had funny patterns carved on the tops of them, some like steps going on either side and some with rows of triangles the way a child might draw mountains. Apart from that, it looked just like a little village clustering on the mountain slope. Nuala could imagine hens pecking around the doorways and toddlers running in and out. It was hard to believe that it was a village built only for the dead.

Just beyond the village, the mountain was cut right back into a great arc, with row upon row of curved steps forming a half-circle.

Kevin let out a shout: 'Look, a stadium! The Nabateans must have played soccer!'

'In this heat?' Nuala gasped, for now that the cliffs had widened the sun was beating down directly on top of them.

'You should have brought your hat,' Kevin told her as they moved on for, unlike him, Nuala's fair skin burned easily. 'Fat people always feel the heat more.'

'I'm not fat,' Nuala snapped, 'and I bet the Nabateans didn't play football. I'd say that place was a theatre.'

'They'd have needed a rock concert to fill a theatre that size,' Kevin commented.

Ahead of them was a great open space where the houses for the living used to stand. By now though, the wind and rain had washed away the soft sandstone bricks. Here the valley was almost as wide as it was long, and the tourists looked like insects as they swarmed around below.

Nuala stopped and mopped her face with a tissue. Immediately fresh sweat broke out again on her forehead and her tongue felt dry in her mouth. This must be how travellers felt crossing the desert, desperate to reach an oasis, she thought.

'I'm terribly thirsty,' she told Kevin. 'D'you think we'd find a stream anywhere?'

'I shouldn't think so,' Kevin said, 'but we can buy coke or something. Mum gave me some money when she changed her travellers' cheque at the Rest House last night. I don't know how much it's worth in Irish money, but I'm sure it will get us a couple of cokes anyway.

'I don't see any shops,' Nuala said. 'Only tombs.'

'All the same, there's bound to be one somewhere,' Kevin assured her. 'They're not going to miss the chance of making money out of all these tourists. They're sure to be flogging coke and postcards and gum and film somewhere. I bet the real reason they widened the Siq was so they could get trucks with supplies in through it!'

Nuala mopped her forehead again, ran her dry tongue round her mouth and stumbled on. Then they saw a building in the distance, standing on its own in the middle of the great open space. Another wall of mountain formed a backdrop behind it, and in front were broken pillars and part of a paved roadway leading towards it.

'It's not cut into the mountain or anything!' Nuala exclaimed in surprise. 'It's just standing there, all on its own, like buildings anywhere else!'

'All the same, it looks very old,' Kevin said. 'You can tell it's really big from the size of the people standing beside it. Look at all the tourists around it! I bet that's the temple.'

'Okay,' Nuala agreed reluctantly. They hadn't come far but she was beginning to feel very hot and tired. Then Kevin clutched her arm in excitement.

'Look,' he exclaimed, 'Over there!'

When she saw where he was pointing, Nuala almost cried with relief. At the base of the cliff to their right was a little hut, surrounded by tables and chairs. Kevin had been right after all. There *was* a café. With the prospect of a cooling drink and a chance to rest her aching legs, Nuala found the energy to hurry down the slope towards it.

When they reached the hut they found a white-robed man wearing one of the red duster head-dresses behind a small counter. Next to him was a large refrigerator, giving out an encouraging hum. An American tourist was buying a coke and, at the sight of it, Kevin's eyes lit up.

'Is this enough for two cokes?' he asked, when it was his turn.

The Bedouin took the handful of coins Kevin held out to him and gave him back a smaller one in place of them.

'Is enough,' he smiled.

He took two bottles from the refrigerator and removed the caps. Gratefully clutching hers to feel the cold against her skin, Nuala carried it out to one of the tables and sank on to a chair. There was a young Arab boy collecting empty bottles from one of the nearby tables and he smiled at her.

'Is very hot,' he said.

'I wonder why you never see any women,' Nuala commented when the boy went into the hut. 'There were no waitresses or barmaids in the Rest House either, only waiters and barmen.'

'I expect they think men are more use,' Kevin grinned, hoping to get a rise out of Nuala, but he was disappointed.

'Women probably have more sense than to work in this heat,' she said, draining the last of her coke and then holding the chilled bottle against her forehead. Only when the bottle was no longer cooler than her skin would she move. Then they set off towards the temple. When they reached it, Nuala stood staring up at the great ruined building, with its huge central arch and crumbling pillars.

'I don't see the dig,' she commented. 'Maybe this isn't the temple at all. We should have asked the man at the café.'

'Can't we ask the guide with that group?' Kevin

suggested, but there was no need, for as they reached the edge of the crowd around him, he was just beginning his speech.

'This is Great Temple of Dhu-Shara,' he was saying. 'Also looks Roman, yes? Notice arches like Roman arches and road to it like Roman road. But is not Roman. Was built by Nabateans about time of birth of Christ, long before Romans conquered city. Was copied from Roman temple, like tombs were copied from Greeks and Assyrians. Was built to honour Nabatean God of Mountains, Dhu-Shara. Shera Mountains take name from him. You can see statue to this god over door of museum ...'

Kevin tugged Nuala's arm.

'Come on,' he said. 'We know now it's the temple. Let's have a look round the back.'

When they got to the far side of the temple they saw a jeep, parked in a tiny patch of shade cast by an overhanging rock. Beside it, a large piece of ground was marked off by stakes stuck into the sandy soil. Twine ran between the stakes and sub-divided the space into several sections. In the middle of one of these sections a group of people squatted on their hunkers. None of them seemed to be digging. They were scraping the ground with pointed trowels or brushing at the loose sand with paintbrushes like so many demented housewives. Nuala knew this had to be the dig. As they got closer, they saw that one person was sieving the sweepings as a cook sieves flour, while another seemed to be putting a small pot carefully into a bath tub. Then Nuala realised that this was her mother.

'Hi, Mum!' she shouted.

Her mother looked up, waved and came over to them.

'Hi!' she said. 'I was afraid you were lost.'

'We stopped for a coke,' Kevin told her. 'You get desperate thirsty in this place.'

'Who are you telling!' his mother replied. 'We brought two huge cans of drinking water with us, and one's empty already. D'you want to see what we're doing?'

'I can see from here,' Kevin said. 'It doesn't look very exciting.'

'It is when you find something.'

'And *have* you found something?'

'Only a couple of pots, but it shows we're digging in the right place. Why don't you have a look round the museum. It's just over there against the mountain. We'll be breaking for lunch in an hour or so.'

'I'd rather explore some of the caves,' Kevin told her.

'So why don't you do that, then? Mr Houston says there's a specially exciting one near here called the

Banqueting Hall, which hardly any tourists get to see because the tour doesn't go that way. Why don't you ask Mr Houston how to find it? He's over there.'

Nuala looked in the direction her mother was pointing. She saw a man squatting on the ground examining something with great excitement.

'Look,' he said to Kevin and Nuala when they went over to him, 'isn't it beautiful?'

All Nuala could see was something like an old two-penny piece that had worn away almost to nothing on one side. Mr Houston brushed it gently with the soft bristles of the brush in his hand and then held it out for her to inspect.

'Look at the picture on it,' he said.

Nuala tilted it slowly so the faded picture engraved on it would show more clearly. Then she laughed.

'It's a camel!' she cried. 'A camel with a saddle on it!'

'A Nabatean coin,' Mr Houston told her, 'used at the time of King Aretas II.'

'Is it worth an awful lot of money?' Kevin asked hopefully.

Mr Houston smiled.

'It's important because it tells us that camels were used by the Nabateans for transport in the year 100 BC,' he said.

Kevin nodded, trying to look interested. 'Mum said

you'd tell us the way to the Banqueting Hall,' he said.

'Sure.' Mr Houston got to his feet and pointed. 'You see that column sticking up over there? The Bedouins call it Amud Fara'un, the Pharaoh's Column, though it has nothing to do with the Pharaohs. Follow the track that runs past it into Wadi Farasa. A little way along you'll see a small cleft in the rock. Climb through it and you'll get a surprise.'

'What sort of surprise?' Nuala asked suspiciously.

'It wouldn't be a surprise if I told you, now would it?' Mr Houston laughed, 'but I promise you it will be a nice one.'

'And is it okay to go without a guide?'

'Sure, only come straight back afterwards. We'll be breaking around midday and we don't want to have to send out a search party.'

Nuala and Kevin followed his directions until they came to the small opening in the rock. It didn't look like the entrance to anywhere, and if Mr Houston hadn't told them to climb through they would never have thought there was a tomb there, especially when all the others they had seen had such large, imposing-looking entrances. Nuala wondered if the original entrance had become blocked by a rock fall from the cliff above. The entrance was so small that it would be impossible for anyone really fat to get through. Kevin darted ahead of her, disappearing through the gap. Then she heard him cry out and felt a sudden chill of fear.

'What is it?' she shouted into the crack, squeezing through after him with difficulty.

Then she too cried out in sheer surprise. They were inside a great hall surrounded by pillars and, between every pillar, the wall was cut back to form an alcove. At the back of the hall, part of one of the alcoves had been cut away, leaving a big black gaping hole, but what made Nuala cry out was the colour. Everything – walls, pillars, alcoves and all – was a deep rich ruby red.

'It's huge!' Kevin gasped. 'Like the great hall at Bunratty!'

'That must be why they call it the Banqueting Hall,' Nuala said. 'But isn't it a fantastic colour?'

Kevin was already inspecting the hole in the back wall.

'What d'you think is through there?' he asked.

'Nothing, probably,' Nuala told him. 'Like at the Treasury.'

'We may as well see,' Kevin said.

'It's dark in there,' Nuala protested. 'It could be full of snakes and those things Mrs Houston warned us about with the sting in their tails.'

'You mean scorpions,' Kevin told her, 'but she said they were in the cracks in the rocks. That's not a crack.

It's a bloody great hole!'

'There aren't any steps up to it,' Nuala argued, 'and it's too high to reach. Besides, you won't see anything in there without a torch.'

'I can easily get up there,' Kevin said, and he proceeded to drag himself up to the ledge and peer in.

'Well?' Nuala asked. 'What can you see?'

'Nothing,' Kevin answered. 'It's too dark, but I think it goes back quite a long way.'

'Do be careful!' Nuala warned, as Kevin began to feel with one foot stretched out ahead of him into the darkness.

'I don't think there's a drop,' he said, inching his way forward and feeling with his left hand along the wall.

Nuala watched anxiously from below, half-expecting at any moment to see him pitch forward into a hole. But he kept moving slowly forward until eventually he disappeared into the darkness.

'What are you doing?' Nuala called after a minute or two. She couldn't see, because her chin didn't quite reach the ledge.

Kevin's words came back muffled and echoing.

'I've reached the back wall,' he said, 'and I can see fine now. It's just a room, like at the Treasury, but there are more alcoves – and there's something on one of these ledges. It looks like a plastic bag. Come and see.'

'I'm not climbing all the way up there just to look at a plastic bag,' Nuala called back. 'And anyway I don't like it when I can't see where I'm going.'

Kevin reappeared on the ledge and stood looking down at her.

'You can see all right when you look back,' he told her, 'and there are no snakes or scorpions. But I want to see what's in that bag and I can't quite reach it. If you came up here I could lift you up to it. Come on, I'll pull you up. Don't be chicken!'

Nuala hated being called a coward and Kevin knew it.

'All right,' she said reluctantly, holding out her arms to him.

Kevin grabbed her hands and, with Nuala using a small groove in the rock to lever herself up with one foot, he hauled her up bodily onto the ledge beside him. Nuala took an uncertain step or two into the darkness ahead, groping with her hands outstretched in front of her.

'It's quite flat,' Kevin reassured her, 'and there's nothing to fall over. Come on!' And he led her into the darkness until she could feel the back wall ahead of her.

'Now,' he ordered, 'turn around and look back.'

When she did so, she could see the rest of the room. As he had told her, it was quite empty, except for a bag on a ledge in the alcove to their left. It was a pink plastic bag and, from the way it was lying, you could tell it was less than half-full. Suddenly she heard a scraping, scrabbling sound and froze in terror, thinking of snakes and rats. Then the sound of a man's voice from outside reassured her. What she had heard was only the sound of someone squeezing in through the hole and scrabbling with their shoes on the rocks. She felt like laughing at her foolishness but Kevin, who was closer to the opening and could see out, clapped a hand over her mouth.

'Don't move or make a sound,' he whispered. 'It's Hassan!'

CHAPTER THREE

The Unseen Gun

Kevin watched as a second man followed Hassan into the Banqueting Hall, but both men moved away from the entrance, out of his view. At the sight of Hassan, both he and Nuala had instinctively shrunk back against the wall. Then Kevin remembered that it was impossible to see into their small chamber, although they could see out of it.

'It's all right,' he whispered to Nuala. 'They can't see us.'

They would be able to hear though, so he remained frozen for fear his feet might scrape the rough sandstone floor and attract their attention. Suddenly he felt an irritation at the back of his throat. Why was it that you always wanted to cough as soon as you knew you mustn't, like in the quiet bits at the school concert? His face burned from the effort of stifling his cough.

He could hear the men's voices but their words

were distorted by echoes and the wall of rock between them. After a while, when the urge to cough had mercifully passed, Kevin went down on all fours and crept slowly, inch by inch, towards the opening. After watching him for a second or two, Nuala did the same. From there the two men were visible.

They were sitting side-by-side on the raised stone ridge bordering the hall, their legs stretched out in front of them. At first Kevin thought they must be speaking Arabic, but then he caught a few words and realised it was only their accents that made their words difficult to understand.

'Ve alvays have given you a fair price,' he heard the other man say, and although the accent was strong it was different from Hassan's and that of the other Bedouins. It reminded him of old war films he had seen on television. He must be German, Kevin decided.

'Now is more difficult.' It was Hassan this time. 'Now archaeologists work here once more.'

'Then perhaps you must vait till they go,' the other man answered. 'Then you vill send vord to the embassy and I vill come back.'

'Money is needed now.'

Kevin could picture the fierce expression on the hawk-like face, though the men's backs were towards him. Hassan was a man who liked to get his own way.

'So vat are you telling me?' Kevin could hear the impatience in the German's voice. 'That ve must pay *more*?'

Hassan flung his arms wide in a shrug.

'I take great risk all times. Jordanian law forbid export of Bedouin treasure. I am Bedouin. We are nomadic race. My people like always to be free. You think I want spend years in gaol? Now risk is greater. For more *risk* must get more *money*.'

The German stood up and Kevin and Nuala instinctively pulled back a little from the opening.

'Then I must speak first vith my ambassador,' he said abruptly. 'I have the authority to pay only vat vas agreed. You give me vat you have now at the old price and I vill make a new price vith my ambassador for the next consignment.'

Hassan got to his feet, shaking his head angrily.

'You talk with ambassador first,' he told him. 'Now I have nothing.'

The German turned to him in disbelief. 'It is now three months since I vas here last,' he said. 'I think you have something but now you vait for more money. That is not honest.'

At that Hassan rounded on him, his eyes blazing. 'Bedouin not slave of German Embassy! I have right to make price for what is mine. Only foolish man poison water of enemy when he must drink from same spring. What you ask is against law of land, yet you say Bedouin not honest! You go now or I take revenge for this insult!'

At this the German, who had already been edging nervously towards the exit, hurriedly squeezed through the gap in the rock and disappeared. Hassan followed him, his words echoing back to the two watchers: 'You speak with ambassador or I find other market!'

Not daring to move or speak for fear he might return, Kevin and Nuala waited for what seemed like ages. Then they both started to speak at once.

'I *knew* he was up to something!' Nuala gasped.

'Now we know why he didn't want us exploring the caves on our own!' Kevin exclaimed. 'I bet he has the treasure hidden in that plastic bag!'

'You couldn't hide much in that,' Nuala scoffed. 'It's too small.'

'You could if it was gold,' Kevin argued. 'Rings and ear-rings and necklaces don't take up much room. Let's find out. I'll lift you so you can reach the bag ...'

'Kevin!'

The call echoed faintly from outside. Then it was repeated.

'Oh, damn! It's Mum!' Nuala cried. 'She'll kill us. We promised we wouldn't be long.'

Kevin cursed. In his excitement he had forgotten

all about his mother.

'This won't take a sec,' he said.

'But they're waiting on us,' Nuala protested. 'Besides, if Mum comes much closer yelling like that the whole of Petra will know where we are and then Hassan will know we heard what he said. Can't we come back after lunch for the bag?'

'Suppose Hassan moves it?'

'Why would he do that? He's waiting for your man to come back with a better offer.'

'Kevin! Nuala!'

The call was nearer now.

'Come on, we have to go,' Nuala said, taking a deep breath and jumping heavily on to the rough floor of the Banqueting Hall.

Kevin hesitated. Then, reluctantly, he followed. The two of them slipped through the crack in the rocks and out into Wadi Farasa.

'Coming, Mum!' Nuala called, to the impatient figure she could see approaching from around a rocky outcrop some fifty yards away.

'For Heaven's sake hurry!' the latter called back. 'Didn't I tell you not to keep Mr Houston waiting?'

'Sorry,' Nuala said, as she got within speaking distance, 'but we got trapped ...' Then she broke off abruptly. How much of what had happened would it be wise to tell their mother?

'D'you mean there was a rock-fall?' her mother asked sharply.

'Not at all. Don't mind Nuala!' Kevin said. 'It was just awkward getting out of the inner cave we were exploring.'

'Well, in future don't go into places you might have trouble getting out of. Maybe it *would* be wiser for you to go around with one of the guides.'

'Oh *no*, Mum!' Kevin protested. 'It wasn't dangerous or anything, honestly. It was just a bit tricky, that's all!'

'Well, next time don't do anything tricky,' his mother told him, 'or I won't be able to let you wander about on your own. You were already warned about rock-falls and snakes and scorpions.'

'But there was nothing like that, Mum,' Kevin pleaded, 'and I'm sorry about being late. We didn't realise how long we'd been.'

'Mr Houston is the one to apologise to,' his mother said, as they reached the jeep. 'You've kept the whole team waiting.'

'It's okay,' said Mr Houston easily. 'You weren't more than five minutes rounding them up. I knew they'd find Petra exciting once they got here. I take it both of you want to come back with us after lunch?'

'Yes, *please*!' Kevin and Nuala chorused.

They went back to the house for lunch to find that Mrs Houston and Amanda had set out salad, bread, cheese, fruit and two big jugs of iced lemonade on the light wooden table in the front room.

'Oh, how lovely!' Kevin's mother exclaimed. 'How much do I owe you?'

'Don't worry about that right now,' Mrs Houston replied. 'We'll have a chat about the housekeeping this evening and sort out our finances. We can put money into a kitty for lunches, I guess.'

'Good idea!' their mother said, pouncing on the jug of lemonade as if she had been travelling across the desert for days. 'But it's not fair for you to have to do all the work.'

'Your turn will come,' Mrs Houston laughed, 'and when it does be sure to wash the salad in bottled water. I meant to tell your kids not to eat unpeeled fruit. If you're taking any with you, be sure you take a knife too.'

'I've got my scout's knife,' Kevin said. 'I can use that.'

As Mr Houston had prophesied, Kevin and Nuala weren't very hungry, though they too were making great inroads on the lemonade. It was odd for Kevin not to be hungry, especially as he had eaten so little the night before. He ate some of the pitta bread with cheese and one of the huge tomatoes, but the slice of sweet juicy melon was what he enjoyed the most. It tasted different from the melon they sometimes had at home, and his mother said it was because it had ripened in the sun instead of being picked green and left to ripen on board a boat or in the wholesaler's.

'Well,' Mrs Houston said while his mother was out making the coffee, 'what did you two get up to all morning?'

'We saw this huge place with great red pillars inside,' Nuala told her.

'Aha!' Mrs Houston exclaimed. 'Chuck's favourite tomb! Did you find it for yourself or did he show it you?'

'He told us where to find it,' Kevin said, adding casually: 'By the way, do the Bedouins have their own special jewellery?'

'They sure do,' Mrs Houston laughed. 'Some of it's very finely worked in low-grade silver, but what looks like ivory may well turn out to be camel bone. I hope you haven't been fooled into spending money on tourist junk.'

'Ah no,' Kevin said, 'we only had just enough to buy coke. But do they have gold and diamonds and things like that?'

Amanda looked at him in the superior way he found so infuriating. 'You shouldn't take any notice of things the Bedouins tell you,' she said. 'They'll say anything to make you buy from them.'

There was no point in asking Amanda and her

mother about the treasure, Kevin thought, and they were the last people he'd choose to confide in.

'Come on, both of you,' his mother ordered as soon as she had drunk her coffee. 'If you're coming back with us this afternoon you must have a rest first. Everyone here takes a siesta in the middle of the day, so you may as well start getting used to it.'

Kevin had thought lying down after lunch was a ridiculous idea when it had first been mentioned, but now he found his eyes were beginning to close. From her tone of voice, he knew his mother was expecting him to protest, but he hadn't the energy. With the shutters drawn all morning, his room was a bit cooler now. He had hardly kicked off his shoes and stretched out on the bed before he fell asleep.

When his mother woke him again, he felt like saying he wouldn't bother going into Petra until the next day. He was hot and sticky, and had hardly enough energy to tie his shoelaces. Then he remembered the pink plastic bag. Jumping out of bed, he splashed cold water on his face and hurried downstairs to the waiting jeep.

It was quite exciting driving through the Siq. The jeep was such a tight fit that Kevin found himself edging inwards on his seat at every twist and turn, as if he were on a ghost train at a funfair. All the same, passing through it at speed didn't give him the same feeling of danger he had got that morning. Mr Houston's voice cut into his thoughts.

'D'you see the channel cut in the rock over there?' he called out, taking one hand off the wheel for a second to point. 'The Nabateans cut that to carry water in from the spring at Wadi Musa. They went to a lot of trouble to install a water system that made their secret city into a fertile, flower-filled valley, although it's surrounded by bare mountains.'

'Why did they go to so much trouble to make their tombs look like palaces?' Kevin asked.

'Probably because of their religion,' Mr Houston explained. 'We don't really know for sure, but they probably believed that when the dead reached the next world, the honour of their welcome would depend on the grandeur of their burial. They also made sacrifices to Dhu-Shara, the god of the mountains.'

'Did they sacrifice animals or people?' Kevin asked, with growing interest.

'We really don't know,' Mr Houston replied. 'There's a basin for holding blood and a drain that carried it down the side of the mountain, which could have served equally well for either.'

'Wow!' Kevin exclaimed.

'You can see the sacrificial altar and the basin and drain for yourself,' Mr Houston continued. 'They're up at the High Place. If you wanna go there this afternoon, I can drop you off before the Necropolis.'

'What's the Necropolis?' Nuala asked, as the jeep emerged from the darkness of the Siq into the light of late afternoon opposite the Treasury, which was now a deep rose red with the rock around it the colour of blackberry juice.

'Where all the smaller tombs are,' her mother told her. 'Just ahead of us now on our left.'

'D'you want me to stop?' Mr Houston asked.

'No, thanks,' Nuala said quickly. 'There's something we have to do this afternoon. We'll go there tomorrow.'

'You see!' her mother said. 'I knew you'd find plenty to do once you were here.' Then she turned to Mr Houston. 'By the way,' she said to him, 'is it my imagination or are our Bedouin helpers very possessive about the Nabateans?'

'You're dead right,' Mr Houston told her. 'They consider themselves the direct descendants of the Nabateans. They're a proud people and, although they're really a nomadic race, this lot have lived here all their lives and their parents and grandparents before them. They look on Petra as their own city. They even lived inside it until it became a tourist attraction. Then the Jordanian government built houses for them at Wadi Musa to get them out of the place.'

'But where did they live before they were moved?' Nuala asked. 'There are no houses here.'

'In the tombs,' Mr Houston explained. 'That's why the government had to move them out.'

'Imagine living in a tomb!' Kevin said, making a face, but Nuala remembered that what Mr Houston called the Necropolis had looked to her like a little mountain village. She thought that she wouldn't have minded living there if all her friends lived there too.

Mr Houston drew up with a jerk at the back of the Temple of Dhu-Shara and called out in Arabic to one of the waiting Bedouins. As they scrambled out, the Bedouin took a tarpaulin from the back of the jeep and threw it over the bonnet.

'There's never any shade at this time of the day,' Mr Houston said, 'and it's not a good idea to let the engine stand in the sun for hours.'

'Don't forget to come back this time,' Kevin's mother said to him as he and Nuala started off towards the Banqueting Hall. 'We'll be leaving as soon as the light goes.'

'It won't take long to see what's in the bag,' Nuala said to Kevin as they passed Pharaoh's Column once more. 'I can't imagine what it is that's worth smuggling, if the Bedouin jewellery is all made from camel bone.'

'You wouldn't want to mind Amanda and her

mother,' Kevin told her. 'They make a jeer out of everything. It must be worth millions if the German Embassy is interested.'

'Maybe we should have told Mum about it,' Nuala said. 'I mean, Hassan even said something about the dig.'

'We'll tell her when we know what it is they're smuggling,' Kevin answered. 'She'll never believe us unless we have something to show her.'

They reached the opening in the rock and Kevin was about to climb through when Nuala gripped his arm.

'Suppose Hassan's in there?' she whispered hoarsely.

'I'll check,' Kevin said, poking a cautious head in through the hole. Then he laughed. 'There's no-one here, come on.'

He darted inside and, with Nuala following more slowly, scrambled up to the inner room.

'It's still there,' he cried triumphantly, returning from the depths to haul Nuala up after him. 'If you stand on my shoulders you should be able to reach it easily.'

He knelt down on the rough floor facing the wall, but Nuala hesitated.

'It'll dirty the shoulders of your T-shirt,' she said.

'So what? Can't it be washed? Hurry up in case someone comes.'

'Your shoulder's too high for me to reach!'

Heaving a patient sigh, Kevin laced his two hands together, holding them against his right hip.

'There's a step for you,' he said.

Trying to take as much of her weight off him as she could by bracing her hands against the wall, Nuala climbed onto his shoulders and raised the bag by its loops. 'It's not very heavy,' she said.

'But *you* are!' Kevin gasped. 'Don't open it up there. Reach it down to me and then jump!'

Nuala passed down the bag, then jumped backwards. She stumbled and fell sideways onto the cave floor. Kevin lowered the bag carefully to the ground and got to his hunkers to examine it, rubbing his knees where the ridges on the cave floor had left a pattern on them. Nuala looked over his shoulder as he parted the pink plastic folds. Then they both cried out in disappointment.

'Just old cracked plates!' Kevin complained. 'And not even gold-plated!'

'They'd have smashed to smithereens if I'd been holding them when I fell,' Nuala commented. 'They're as thin as egg-shells.'

'What harm if they had!' Kevin cried in disgust. 'They're only rubbish. Look, they're chipped as well as cracked.'

'They're pretty all the same,' said Nuala. 'A lovely

tomato red with a funny black leaf-pattern on them.'

'They can be sky-blue-pink for all I care!' Kevin retorted. 'They're not Bedouin treasure.'

'I wonder who they belong to?' Nuala said. 'We'd better put them back where we found them.'

'If you think I'm going to let a big fat lump like you climb all over me again, just for the sake of some cracked plates, you're more cracked than they are!' Kevin snapped. 'Just dump them any old where.'

'All right. I'll put them here in the corner,' Nuala said, hurt. 'No-one will trip over them there.'

'I wouldn't lose sleep over it if they did,' Kevin told her. 'Come on. Let's go.'

It was a silent, disappointed pair that left the Banqueting Hall and followed the track back along Wadi Farasa towards Pharaoh's Column.

'What are we going to do now?' Nuala asked. 'They'll be ages at the dig before it's time to go.'

'I suppose we might as well take a look at the museum,' Kevin suggested. 'It's probably a dead bore, but it's too hot to tramp all the way across the valley to look at those big tombs all the tourists keep going to. Mum said the museum was quite near.'

'I think that must be it,' Nuala told him, pointing, 'where all the bits of broken pillars are stacked behind the steps.'

'You mean over there, the cave with the statue over

the door? Looks like just another old tomb.'

'It probably is. Isn't the restaurant at the Rest House in a tomb? I bet the museum's in one too.'

'People around here seem to spend their lives in tombs,' Kevin said, as they headed for the building Nuala had pointed out, 'but I suppose it saves the cost of moving them to one when they die!'

They were near the museum when a small figure that Kevin had noticed from a distance ever since they had reached the open valley came close enough for them to see clearly. It was a boy, not much shorter than Kevin but a great deal skinnier. He had silky black hair and dark brown skin, and wore a faded blue denim shirt and jeans. Over his back was slung an old-fashioned school satchel. As soon as he came within earshot, he gave them a large toothy grin and shouted a greeting.

'Good-morning-how-are-you?' he called out in one sentence, as if reciting an exercise in class.

'It's not morning any more, it's evening,' Kevin laughed. 'But how did you know we speak English?'

'Only English have white skin and nothing on head,' the boy replied, laughing too.

'Well, we're not English, so there!' Kevin told him. 'We're Irish, but we *speak* English.'

'I-rish?' the boy repeated, puzzled. 'What country?'

'Ireland,' Nuala explained. 'Next door to England.

Have you been at school?'

'School,' he repeated again, nodding. 'But now holidays.'

'You mean, you've just broken up for the summer?' Kevin exclaimed. 'But you came from up there!' And he pointed across the valley. A track led up the mountains beyond the row of large tombs, surrounded by a crowd of tourists. 'I was watching you.'

'School up there,' the boy nodded. 'In cave.'

'Wow!' Nuala gasped. 'They even go to school in tombs here.'

'Not tomb. Cave,' the boy said. 'Live in cave also. Over there,' and he pointed towards the distant cliffs behind them to the south-west.

'You mean, your home is a *cave*?' Nuala asked.

The boy nodded. 'Like see?'

'I certainly would,' said Kevin.

'Then come,' the boy answered, and added, as an afterthought, 'my name Ali.'

'Hi, Ali,' Kevin replied. 'I'm Kevin and this is Nuala.'

At that moment, a large group of tourists came down the steps from the museum, chattering in some foreign language. In the midst of them was the tall figure of Hassan. Kevin pulled Nuala by the arm.

'Don't let him see you,' he urged.

Ali looked at Kevin curiously as the three of them hurried away.

'You not like?' he asked.

'Not much,' Kevin told him. 'Do *you* like him?'

Ali suddenly became very serious. 'Him bad man,' he said with emphasis. 'Under his shirt he have gun. Ali has seen. One time man make Hassan angry and Hassan kill. Is good you stay away from him.'

Maybe it was just as well they hadn't found any Bedouin treasure, thought Nuala. There was no knowing what a man like Hassan might do to someone who got in his way. Even in the heat of the late afternoon sun, she found herself shivering at the thought of how close they had already been to danger.

CHAPTER FOUR

The Bedouin Treasure

Ali led Kevin and Nuala towards another cliff face to the south-west.

'Those rocks are almost orange!' Nuala gasped.

Ali laughed. 'All Petra like orange soon,' he told her. 'Then all gold.'

'So the rocks really do change colour,' Kevin exclaimed. 'I thought that was just travel brochure stuff.'

'Can tell time by colour,' Ali said. He pointed ahead of them to a cave mouth from which smoke was drifting. 'This my home. Mother make bread.'

'But how do you tell people where you live?' Nuala asked, wondering what possible address you could give if you lived in a cave.

'That Umm al Biyara,' Ali told her, pointing to the cliff. 'You say you meet Ali from Umm al Biyara and all people know.'

As they came closer to the cave, a wonderful smell

made Nuala's nostrils twitch. Now she could see a small dark woman kneeling beside the smoking fire. She wore a black tunic, embroidered along the hem and at the fastenings with red flowers on a green lacy stem. She had a black scarf twisted around her head which fell over her shoulders and down her back. She was bent over a floury board laid on the cave floor, with her yellow-sleeved arms outstretched, kneading a small ball of dough between her two hands.

Nuala stopped, fascinated, as the woman dipped one hand into a white enamel bowl of water beside her. She flattened the ball of dough, and then stretched it swiftly backwards and forwards between her hands until it hung from one hand like a curtain of thin white material. Then she flung this on to a round metal sheet balanced across the hot logs of the fire. Hardly had it touched the darkened metal than it turned a golden brown and she at once snatched it up again, flinging it on to the curling pile at the end of the board. Now it looked like a thinner version of the pitta bread, except that it was only a single sheet instead of being in the envelope shape into which Nuala had shovelled hummus at dinner the previous night.

'Mmm!' Nuala said appreciatively, 'it smells only gorgeous!'

At the sound of her voice, the woman looked up

and smiled. She spoke softly in Arabic to Ali, who answered her in the same language and pushed Nuala and Kevin closer to the cave mouth.

'Wel-come,' the woman said to them. 'You like eat?'

Nuala felt that people living in caves might not have a lot of food to be sharing with strangers. On the other hand, it might offend Ali's mother if she refused. In any case, the smell was very tempting.

'You try?' the woman suggested, holding out the piece she had just thrown on to the board.

'Thanks,' Nuala said, taking it, breaking it in half and giving one of the halves to Kevin. She put the warm bread into her mouth and gave a cry of delight. 'Oh, it's fantastic!'

'Deadly!' Kevin agreed enthusiastically. 'Much nicer than that old stuff they had in the Rest House.'

'It's so clever, the way you do it,' Nuala said, 'and you do it so fast.'

'If slow bread burn,' the woman laughed. 'Look. I show you!'

She scooped up another ball of dough, wetted it with water from the bowl and rolled it between her hands.

'Come,' she said to Nuala.

Nuala put her foot on the stone that was like a doorstep up to the cave and climbed into it. Then she squatted down on her hunkers between Ali's mother and a large pot which was keeping warm in the ashes of the fire.

His mother called out something in Arabic to Ali. He dumped his school bag somewhere in the recesses of the cave, fetched a plastic bucket from a ledge and, calling to Kevin to go with him, set off up the wadi. It seemed that the Bedouins still considered cooking to be women's work, but Nuala supposed you could hardly expect people living in caves to be progressive about things like that.

Ali's mother took Nuala's two hands, laughing, and put them down in the flour, moving them until they were coated in it. Then she handed her a ball of dough. Nuala flattened it on the board the way she had seen Ali's mother do it and began to try to stretch it, but almost at once it started to tear.

Laughing again, the woman took it back from her and rolled and flattened it once more. Then, using Nuala's hands as if they were kitchen implements, she tossed the dough backwards and forwards, stretching it little by little all the time, until the white curtain hung over Nuala's bare arm. Carefully, Nuala swung her arm so that the stretched dough fell on the hot metal sheet over the fire, but it was Ali's mother who snatched it back as it turned crisp and golden. Then she dipped water on to the pile of flour to make some dough.

'Now you!' she said to Nuala encouragingly.

Nuala scooped up a handful of dough, rolled it into a ball, flattened it and very slowly began to stretch it out.

Meanwhile, Kevin and Ali had followed the wadi until the tinkling of bells made Ali turn sharply to his right. There, behind a projecting rock, Kevin saw three goats munching happily away at a miserable stump of prickly cactus.

'Don't they mind the prickles?' he asked.

'Goat eat anything,' Ali answered with a smile.

To Kevin's surprise, Ali squatted on the rock and, talking to the first goat in Arabic all the while, proceeded to milk her. The goat made a playful attempt to butt him with her head, and Ali laughed and held her away from him by the horns. After that the goat went back to munching the cactus and ignored him. Kevin had once seen a cow milked by hand, when the Dairy Council had given a special demonstration at the RDS during the Spring Show. Two of the cows had been milked by machine, while the third was milked by hand. All the same, Kevin found the very idea of milking a goat funny, but he stopped laughing when Ali said: 'Now you!'

Even though Ali held the second goat by her horns so she couldn't even try to butt him, Kevin was unable to get milk from the udders. While still holding her with one hand, Ali stretched the other in under her belly and showed him how to squeeze the milk downwards, instead of pulling on the teats as he had been doing. In the end he got the knack of it. He didn't get as much milk from her as Ali had done from the first goat though, and Ali had to finish her off, as well as milking the third goat himself. All the same, when they got back with the bucket of warm milk, Kevin shouted triumphantly: 'I milked one of the goats myself!'

'And I made three pieces of bread all by myself,' Nuala announced for her part, 'and the last piece I even took off the fire by myself!'

By now the heap of flour was gone, and there was a large pile of bread on the board in its place. A kettle sang on the smoking fire where the hot metal baking sheet had been. Ali's mother motioned them to sit around the fire while she made the tea, stirring the sugar directly into the pot.

'*Shaii*?' she asked, pointing to the tea and Nuala repeated the word after her as she nodded her head.

'Now you speak Arabic,' Ali laughed, as his mother poured the tea for her and Kevin.

'How do you say "Thank you"?' Nuala asked.

'*Shukran*,' Ali told her.

'*Shukran*,' Nuala repeated as she accepted a plastic cup of the hot, scalding liquid.

'Ow! It's boiling!' Kevin cried at the first sip and he accepted a little of the goats' milk, scooped straight from the bucket in a plastic jug, to cool it.

Nuala did the same, though she noticed that both Ali and his mother drank their tea without milk. It tasted very sweet and a little strange with warm goat's milk in it instead of the chilled and pasteurised cows' milk they got at home, but for once Kevin didn't complain. After all, it was milk that he had produced by his own labour!

They were still sipping the scalding tea when they saw a man and a boy coming up the wadi towards them. Kevin at once recognised the man who had sold him the two cokes that morning. Ali and his mother stood up to make room for them beside the fire as they called out a greeting, so Nuala and Kevin rose also.

'This my father,' Ali said, as the man smiled at them with a flash of white, gapped teeth.

'We meet already,' the man said, 'at Bedouin tea place.'

'I see you also,' the other boy grinned and Nuala realised it was he who had been clearing the empty bottles from the tables.

'My brother Hani,' Ali explained. 'He finish school already. Work now with my father.'

Ali's mother bustled about, getting plastic bowls,

and Nuala guessed the meal was going to consist of something more than bread and tea. The large pot she had noticed earlier was moved directly above the fire in place of the kettle. It was the family mealtime, while tea could be offered to guests at any time of day.

'We must go,' Nuala said.

'You welcome eat with us,' Ali's father replied courteously.

'*Shukran*,' Nuala replied gravely, 'but there will be a meal for us at Wadi Musa and my mother will be waiting. She said to be back before the light goes.'

Even as she spoke she realised that the wall of the cliff opposite was a dull gold colour, and that the sun was sinking fast behind the mountain.

'But you come tomorrow?' Ali inquired anxiously.

'Sure,' Kevin replied easily, 'then we can go to the High Place.'

'Tomorrow,' Ali's father stated, 'Ali must take goats to Al-Deir.'

'I promise Kevin,' Ali protested. 'I tell him now is holiday.'

'You take holiday next day,' his father said, shrugging.

Ali looked sullen. 'You shame me before friend,' he sulked.

'Take friend to Al-Deir,' his mother suggested.

'Kevin not like minding goats.'

'You show him Monastery. Take him to High Place later.'

'He not want spend all day with me.'

'I wouldn't mind at all,' Kevin told him. 'We could bring a picnic. It might be a lot of fun.'

'Please, what is pic-nic?' asked Ali's mother.

'Any meal at all,' Nuala explained, 'when you have it outdoors somewhere.'

'I make pic-nic,' Ali's mother said. 'You like hummus?'

'I think it's yummy,' Nuala said, nodding with such enthusiasm that her words needed no translation.

'Then I make pic-nic with hummus. Okay?'

'If you're sure it wouldn't be too much trouble,' Nuala said politely.

Ali's mother shook her head, laughing. 'Make picnic for Ali when he take goats. Now make for you also.'

'Thanks a million,' Nuala cried, 'I mean, *shukran*.'

'But will Mum let us?' Kevin asked her. 'We'll have to ask my mother first,' he explained to the family.

'Ali,' ordered his father. 'You go speak with mother.'

'But what about your dinner?' Nuala asked Ali as he jumped down out of the cave immediately.

'Is hot in pot,' Ali laughed. 'Come!'

'Goodbye, then. See you tomorrow!' Nuala said,

and she could hear the others echoing her words as she and Kevin followed Ali back down the wadi towards the dig.

'Why do the goats have to go to this place in the morning?' Kevin asked Ali when he caught up with him. 'What are they going to do to them there?'

'Is no-one at Al-Deir,' Ali told him. 'Only my uncle have cave there.'

'So why do the goats have to go to your uncle?'

'No, no!' Ali shook with laughter. 'Not go to uncle. Go for food. Al-Deir is high up mountain. More grows for goats eating.'

'But why do you have to stay all day with them? Couldn't you just take them there and leave them?'

'Goats not safe by their own. Go too far or bad man steal. Must watch all time.'

'But you don't watch them all the time here.'

'Here can see all time. Or hear bells. If no hear bells, go look.'

'But couldn't you take them up the mountains and then tie them by a long rope so they couldn't wander?'

'Must move all time for food.'

'It's not like at home,' Nuala pointed out to Kevin, 'where you could tie them in a field with grass all round them. Here there's only a bit of cactus here and a small bit of tree growing somewhere else. They'd have to keep moving about to get enough grazing.'

'Nuala know,' Ali laughed. 'Goats also want holiday!'

They were close to the dig now, but Kevin could see no sign of his mother. There were only Bedouin helpers, carrying soil to tip on to a pile to one side or collecting up the little pointed trowels.

'D'you know where my mother is?' he asked the man who had put the tarpaulin over the bonnet of the jeep.

'In museum,' the man replied, waving his arm towards the doorway at the top of the steps.

'What's that statue over the door?' Kevin asked Ali, as they went towards it.

'Is Dhu-Shara, god of mountains,' Ali told him. 'Found on ground near temple.'

'His face looks kind of washed away,' Kevin commented.

'But I love his woolly beard,' Nuala said, 'and he looks kind. He's staring far away like he's watching over everything in his kingdom.'

'I don't know what he can watch with those eyes,' Kevin argued. 'They look like the eyes of a blind man.'

'Maybe gods don't need eyes to see,' Nuala said, as they climbed the top step. They passed under the statue and in through the open door of the museum.

As they went in, Nuala had a sudden fear that Hassan might be there with more tourists, but there was no-one at all peering into the glass cases.

'Not many customers here this evening,' Kevin remarked, as he glanced around him.

'Tourists all gone home now,' Ali told him.

'But where's Mum?' Nuala asked.

'Inside in the office, I suppose,' Kevin said, pointing to a door marked PRIVATE with Arabic writing above it. 'Shall I knock?'

'I suppose so,' Nuala said doubtfully, but Kevin was already rapping loudly on the door.

A voice called out something he could not catch, so he stuck his head around the edge of the door. His mother and Mr Houston were sitting with their backs to him, facing across a broad desk to where a dark-skinned man with iron-grey hair sat in a swivel chair. The man looked at Kevin inquiringly.

'I'm sorry to interrupt,' Kevin began, 'but …'

At the sound of his voice, his mother turned her head.

'Wait for me outside, Kevin, please,' she said crisply. 'I won't be five minutes.'

'Okay,' Kevin said reluctantly, closing the door again. 'I hope you're not too hungry,' he said to Ali, 'because we've got to wait.'

'Is okay,' Ali assured him, going to sit on the bench under the window.

Kevin joined him, and Nuala wandered about,

looking at the things in the glass cases. She didn't find them terribly interesting. They seemed to be all broken bits and pieces. There were bits of broken pillars like those stacked outside, broken pots and pieces of statues. Over at the far side of the room was a case full of bowls and jugs, though she couldn't figure out how they stayed upright when they weren't on special stands, because they were pointed underneath. Then she saw a flash of red, the exact same dark tomato red as the cracked plates they had found in the pink plastic bag.

When she went closer she cried out in surprise, for these too were plates. You could see that they had been broken and put together again – there were still little white triangles in one of them where bits of the glazing had chipped off, showing the natural colour of the clay before it had been painted. There were two plates with the same pattern of black leaves on that familiar dark tomato-red background.

Kevin and Ali came over to see what she was staring at.

'I don't believe it!' Kevin gasped, when he saw the plates. 'Someone has glued them together and put them in a case!'

'They're not the same ones, you clown,' Nuala said. 'These must have been here for ages. Look, they're all dusty, and so are the stands and labels. You don't think someone stuck them together and labelled them and found stands to put them on and everything since we left the Banqueting Hall do you?'

'But why do they want to show people broken plates?' Kevin wondered aloud.

'Because they're *old*,' Nuala said. 'Like the things in Mum's museum in Dublin that were found at Wood Quay. They've got broken plates there too.'

'That's true,' Kevin agreed, 'and most of the other things here seem to be broken or chipped. But if they have them in glass cases it must mean they're valuable.'

Ali nodded in agreement.

'People pay much money for these things,' he said.

'And you thought the plates we found this morning were only old rubbish!' Nuala told Kevin. 'You said it wouldn't matter if they got smashed up! Aren't you glad now that I put them down carefully in the corner where no-one would fall over them?'

'But are they *really* worth a lot?' Kevin asked Ali incredulously.

'Nabatean pottery very good,' Ali told him. 'Is Bedouin treasure.'

'Bedouin treasure!' Kevin echoed. 'You mean we found the Bedouin treasure after all? So that's what Hassan was trying to flog and we never even put it back on the shelf!'

CHAPTER FIVE

The View From the Cave

Nuala looked at Kevin in dismay. 'We must go back and get it at once,' she said.

'You're not going anywhere ...' her mother's voice cut in from behind her. 'We're finished here now. Whatever it is will have to wait till tomorrow.'

'That may be too late!' Kevin wailed.

'It can't be helped,' his mother answered in the voice that Kevin knew by now meant she wasn't really listening. 'Mr Houston is ready to go and we mustn't keep him waiting a second time.'

'But this is really important,' Nuala pleaded. 'You'll want to see it yourself, because it's to do with archaeology.'

'I'm delighted to hear you're finally taking an interest in archaeology,' her mother replied, walking briskly towards the door. 'You can tell me all about it this evening over dinner.'

'But Ali went without his dinner to come and talk to you!' Nuala cried, running after her, 'and it's not *his* fault that you were talking to the museum man and couldn't be interrupted.'

'Who's Ali?' her mother asked, hesitating in mid-stride.

'Is me,' Ali said. 'And I ask permission that Kevin and Nuala come to Al-Deir tomorrow.'

'Al-Deir?' their mother echoed, confused at the new direction the conversation was taking.

'The temple known as the Monastery,' said the museum director, who was waiting by the door to lock up after them. 'It's in the mountains above Petra. It's well worth a visit if you have time to go.'

'Is it far?' their mother asked. 'I mean, will they be all right there on their own?'

'They don't have to go outside Petra,' the director told her, 'and if they're going with Ali they won't get lost.'

'How long will it take them?'

She directed her question to the director, but it was Kevin who answered.

'We'll be gone all day,' he said, 'because Ali has to mind the goats, but his mother's packing us a picnic lunch and she sent Ali to ask if it would be all right.'

'The parents live up at Umm al Biyara,' the director said helpfully. 'A very respectable family. The father runs the Bedouin tea kiosk and the elder son gives him a hand with it, but Ali here is still at school.'

'Only now is holidays,' Ali added.

'So if the parents know about the arrangements I think you could safely give permission,' the director finished.

'Oh, all right then,' their mother said, 'provided you're back in good time to come home with us in the evening.'

'But tomorrow my father bring empty bottles to Wadi Musa,' Ali said. 'Can bring them also.'

Again their mother turned to the museum director for guidance.

'Do you think that's advisable?' she asked.

'I'm sure you can rely on them,' he told her. 'Ali's father will have to pick up his supplies for the big tourist invasion at the weekend.'

'Very well then,' she said finally, hurrying off down the steps.

'But what about the Bedouin treasure?' Kevin persisted, following her, but she only snapped: 'That's enough now. You've got your permission. You can tell me the rest at dinner.'

Then she climbed into the jeep and Kevin and Nuala had no choice but to do the same. They said goodbye to Ali, and he headed off towards home and his dinner.

'Wouldn't it make you sick?' Kevin whispered to Nuala as they drove back through the Siq. 'To think we had the treasure in our hands!'

'We'll have to try and get to it before we go to the Monastery,' Nuala whispered back.

'If Mum would only listen!' Kevin moaned. 'She's impossible when she's thinking about her work!'

'She'll be mad with herself when she finds out what it's about,' Nuala told him. But it took some time to convince their mother that they hadn't dreamed the whole thing.

'As if anyone would leave Nabatean pottery lying around in a plastic bag!' she scoffed.

'But he was hiding it,' Kevin argued, 'to give to the man from the German Embassy as soon as he could get him to up the price.'

'I can't see any embassy lending itself to that class of carry-on,' his mother replied. 'Taking goods of archaeological significance out of the country carries very heavy penalties under Jordanian law.'

'I'm not so sure,' Mr Houston said thoughtfully. 'An embassy would have a better chance of getting away with it, because the customs don't see what goes out in diplomatic baggage.'

'But where would the likes of this Bedouin get Nabatean pottery?' their mother demanded.

'You've gotta remember,' Mr Houston told her, 'that

Petra has never been properly excavated. The only archaeological team here before us was German. Most of the stuff in the museum comes from that dig, so the German connection makes a lot of sense. The Germans would have used Bedouin helpers as we do and this guy Hassan could have been one of them. He could have learned then what was valuable and where to look for it, so what was to stop him carrying on in his own time under his own steam after the team left? The contacts he made at the embassy during the dig would be the obvious channel for his finds.'

'Then we must put a stop to it at once!' their mother cried indignantly. 'Nabatean pottery is too rare to let it all go into private collections in Germany for this man's personal gain.'

'First we gotta get hold of this bag the kids found and take a look at its contents,' Mr Houston said. 'I vote we go to the Banqueting Hall tomorrow first thing, before we start work on the dig. And, in the meantime, say nothing about this to anyone.'

So, feeling very important, Kevin and Nuala led the way the next morning to the Banqueting Hall. Their mother was as impressed as they had been with the Hall itself and its ruby red pillars.

'I suppose,' she said to Mr Houston, 'those niches originally held the statues of their gods.'

'Could be,' he agreed, 'or maybe urns containing

the ashes of their dead. But just look at the perfection of those chiselled pillars and the ribboned ornamentation of that ceiling!'

'The colour pattern's like a modern painting!'

'Yeah, but it's entirely natural. This red sandstone contains amazing colour gradations.'

'Never mind all that,' cried Kevin impatiently, climbing up on to the ledge of the inner room. 'Wait till you see the plates.'

He groped his way forward, unable to see anything, until his body no longer blocked the light from the opening.

'Mind you don't trip over them!' Nuala called after him anxiously. 'I left them down on the floor, remember!'

'I know that!' Kevin's voice echoed back to them from the inner room.

His outstretched hand felt the wall and he swung eagerly around, but there was no pink plastic bag in the corner where Nuala had put it.

'It's gone!' he called out in dismay.

'Maybe someone put it back up on the shelf,' Nuala suggested.

'I'm not blind,' Kevin shouted back angrily. 'I tell you it's gone!'

'Are you quite sure you didn't dream up the whole thing?' his mother asked, as Kevin dropped disconsolately to the floor of the Banqueting Hall.

'Of course I'm sure!' he raged. 'And it's all your fault. Didn't I tell you last night we shouldn't leave it till today, but you wouldn't listen!'

'Someone must have got here before us,' Nuala said gloomily.

'Let's hope it was someone who knew its worth,' her mother commented, 'and will hand it over to the museum.'

'I wouldn't bet on it!' Mr Houston said dryly. 'Its worth around here might mean how many dollars can be got for it, especially if it was our friend Hassan.'

'It probably *was* Hassan,' Nuala groaned. 'Hardly anyone seems to come in here, apart from him and us.'

Then a dreadful thought struck her. She waited until their mother and Mr Houston had gone back to the dig and they were on their way to Ali's place in Umm al Biyara before telling Kevin about it.

'I didn't want to say this in front of Mum,' she said then, 'in case she didn't let us go with Ali, but we're in real trouble now.'

'Who are you telling?' Kevin replied sulkily. 'It was stinking bad luck losing the lousy old treasure.'

'It's worse than that,' Nuala pointed out. 'Don't you see? If Hassan took it he'll know that we know about it.'

'How? He never saw us at the Banqueting Hall.'

'No, but he'll know *someone* knows. If we'd put the bag back where we found it, it might still be there, but when Hassan discovered it on the floor, he must have known someone had looked at it. That's why he took it away.'

'So what? There's no way he could have known it was us.'

'No, but he'll be dead suspicious of everyone now. He's probably moved it to another hiding place, but if he catches us poking around in all the other caves, he'll know we're hunting for it.'

'We can't look in all the other caves anyway. There's millions of them!'

'But we're here for weeks! We could look at a few every day,' Nuala insisted.

'Yeah,' said Kevin, 'only now we'll have to be dead careful. If Hassan sees us he'll come after us, and you heard what Ali said about him.'

They stopped talking about it then but, when they reached Ali's cave, there was Ali with a pink plastic bag in his hand.

'It was *you* who took the treasure!' Kevin shouted with glee, hurrying towards him.

Ali looked at him, puzzled and a little hurt.

'I take nothing,' he said.

'So what's that?' Kevin asked, pointing to the bag in his hand.

'This pic-nic,' Ali told him. 'Hummus and bread and Coca-Cola from Bedouin tea place.'

'Everything you buy in Wadi Musa must come in pink plastic bags,' Nuala said.

'Pity!' Kevin exclaimed. 'For a moment there I thought Ali had saved the day.'

As they rounded up the goats and began to drive them up the wadi, he told Ali the whole story and Ali's big brown eyes widened.

'Hassan very bad man,' he repeated. 'You no look for treasure now. Is too dangerous.'

'Oh well,' Kevin said, 'let's forget about it for now. Do your goats have names?'

'This Allat,' Ali said, slapping the back of the largest of the three goats. 'This Fatima and this daughter of Fatima. Call her El-Bint. Means daughter.'

'And do they answer to their names?' Nuala asked.

'When call, all come,' Ali laughed and gave a strange piercing cry. At once the goats ran over to him, nuzzling his hand as if hoping for food.

'Oh, they think you've got something for them,' Nuala cried reproachfully, but Ali only laughed again.

'They get plenty food at Al-Deir,' he said.

It was a long, steep climb, some of it over worn steps cut into the rocks, some over rough tracks of sand and gravel winding around the cliffs, but always ascending. The goats pattered on ahead of them, sure-footed even on the sharpest and most slippery slopes. They lingered over gnarled juniper trees projecting from the cliffs, which they munched in delight until Ali called them on again with his sharp cry. They crossed narrow footbridges over deep ravines, and several times Nuala begged Ali to stop while she rested for a few minutes on a rock.

The further they went, the fewer people they saw, even in the distance. By the time they began skirting the mountain that Ali told them was Jebel Al-Deir, they saw no-one at all except one fat Bedouin astride a small donkey, the hem of his white robes almost sweeping the ground as the donkey crossed the track ahead of them.

'How on earth can he ride up there?' Nuala cried, as the donkey picked its way carefully up a steep flight of shallow steps leading right up to a shoulder of the mountain.

'Him Bedouin,' Ali shrugged and Nuala realised that Ali considered that sufficient explanation for any display of skill.

Finally they reached the pass, and the goats raced on ahead, scenting the sweet oleander. Following more slowly, Kevin suddenly saw the Monastery of Al-Deir.

'It's huge!' he gasped. 'Bigger even than the Treasury.'

'Is wider,' Ali agreed, 'but five feet shorter.'

'It doesn't *look* shorter,' Nuala argued.

'Because urn on top very big,' Ali told her. 'This urn twenty-seven feet high. Also, Al-Deir not set into rock like Treasury.'

'You're right!' Kevin exclaimed. 'This one was built properly, like the Temple of Dhu-Shara.'

Ali shook his head. 'No, is carved from one big rock,' he explained.

'We may as well take a look inside,' Kevin said, with a meaningful glance at Nuala.

'You look,' Ali told him. 'I watch goats.'

So Kevin and Nuala stepped up from the sandy valley on to the raised sandstone floor. They went in through the doorway, set in the centre of the eight pillars carved along its façade. It seemed dark inside after the dazzling morning sunlight in the wadi, but their eyes soon adjusted to the lack of light. They saw it was like the Treasury and the Banqueting Hall, one main room with niches around it. It had none of the splendours of the Banqueting Hall, though. There were no carved pillars, only a simple room like that of a small country church. It did have an alcove at the back, but this one was like a separate inner room. It was quite large and had a lower entrance with a step leading up to it. Kevin glanced across at Nuala.

'I bet people hardly ever come this far,' he said. 'I

mean it took us ages to get here.'

They both hurried eagerly into the little room but there was no pink plastic bag or, indeed, anything else except a small bare altar at the back.

'It was stupid to expect it,' Nuala said, fighting her disappointment. 'Why should it be in the one place we happened to go?'

'Because it's so far from anywhere,' Kevin said. 'But it can't be helped. We'll just have to go on looking. Let's go.'

They found Ali a little further up the wadi. The goats were devouring the small clumps of green shrubs which were scattered around all over the place.

'It's lovely up here,' Nuala said, looking at the mountains ahead and the cliffs on either side. 'There's even a teeny-weeny bit of a breeze.'

'Is cold at night,' Ali told her. 'You hungry?'

'Thirsty,' she answered. 'My mouth and lips are so dry I feel as if they're going to crack open.'

'I'm hungry *and* thirsty,' Kevin said. 'Look, the sun's nearly overhead now. It must be coming on midday.'

'Goats have pic-nic,' Ali laughed. 'Now we have ours. Come.' He walked off towards the cliffs opposite the Monastery.

'Where are we going?' Kevin wanted to know, as he and Nuala followed.

'Cave,' Ali said, and then they saw the black hole,

high in the cliff-face. Using a rock as a stepping stone, Ali climbed into it.

'Why is it so high up?' Nuala asked, struggling to follow him. 'It's much higher than the one you live in.'

'Keep out animals and snakes,' Ali told her. 'Many snakes at Al-Deir.'

'Yuk!' Nuala said. 'Are you sure there are none in here?' and she peered uneasily into the cave.

'No snakes here,' Ali laughed, and then Nuala noticed that this cave was furnished, with thick Bedouin rugs on the floor. There were candles, matches, plastic beakers and a jug and bowl neatly stacked on a ledge.

'Who do all these things belong to?' she asked.

'Belong my uncle,' Ali said. 'Is for guests. Sit now.'

Nuala pulled herself up into the cave with an effort. She sank gratefully onto the soft rugs, kicking off her shoes.

'That's better,' she sighed, as Ali handed her a bottle of coke.

'How did you manage to keep it so cool?' she exclaimed in delight.

'Take from ice at Bedouin tea place,' Ali explained. 'Then wrap in much paper.'

'It's deadly!' Kevin said. 'Now, where's that hummus?'

Ali took out a large screw-top jar full of hummus and a pile of bread, and put it all on the cave floor, with the pink plastic bag as a tablecloth. The bread was rather dry and not as nice as when it had been freshly baked by Ali's mother, but it was easier dipping it into the hummus than if it had been softer, and nobody complained. While they ate, Ali kept one eye on the goats, calling them back if they went too far, and the minute he had finished eating he jumped to his feet.

'Now take goats higher,' he said. 'More oleander there.'

'Oh!' Nuala exclaimed. 'Must we? I'm bunched!'

'It's our siesta time,' Kevin said grandly, lolling back on the rugs.

'So sleep,' Ali said. 'I take goats. Come back in one–two hours' time.'

'Okay,' Nuala said. She watched Ali collect the empty coke bottles, the jar that had held the hummus and the layers of paper used to keep everything cool, replacing them all in the pink plastic bag. Then he put the bag on the cave ledge and jumped to the ground.

It had been a long stiff climb, and Nuala felt drowsy in the heat. She pulled herself deeper into the cave to make sure all of her was in the shade. It would be dangerous, she knew, to fall asleep in the sun.

'Mind you don't burn while you sleep,' she said to Kevin, who was already nodding. He waved her warning away with one hand as if it were a troublesome fly, but he did swing his legs around so that his whole body was further from the mouth of the cave.

Ali had disappeared from sight, but she could hear his voice calling to the goats and the tinkling of their bells growing fainter in the distance as she dozed off.

Nuala woke up, trying to remember at first where she was. Then she felt the soft Bedouin rug beneath her bare arms, and she could smell the oleander outside the cave. She rolled over and saw Kevin lying beside her. He hadn't stirred.

She struggled to a sitting position and began to put on her shoes. Looking out of the cave mouth from the position she was in, she could see only the Monastery and the small bit of wadi directly between it and the cave, framed like a picture by the cave opening. There was no sign of Ali or the goats. She would have to go right to the lip of the cave to find out if they were coming.

As she put her hands onto the cave floor to lever herself to her feet a movement opposite caught her eye. A man in white Bedouin robes was coming out the doorway of the Monastery. Quickly she shrank back further into the depths of the cave, for there was no mistaking the tall figure and hawk-like nose of Hassan.

CHAPTER SIX

The High Place

Hassan looked quickly to right and left, and then set off towards the city. To Nuala's relief, he glanced only casually in her direction. It was clear he couldn't see into the darkness of the cave, as only the stepping-stone rock was now in direct sunlight. From his behaviour, Nuala guessed Ali and the goats must also be out of sight, so it must not yet be two hours since they had left.

She was tempted to dash straight across to the Monastery to see if the pink plastic bag was there, for she could think of no other reason for Hassan's visit. But she restrained herself. In the silence of Al-Deir, a sudden flurry of movement might be heard from a distance and cause him to look back.

As she fought her impatience, it occurred to her that it might be as well that Ali wasn't around while they sought the treasure. He had seemed so anxious that they shouldn't tangle with Hassan. On the other hand, if they did find it, they could hardly return with a second pink plastic bag without his noticing. She looked at the one Ali had left sitting on the cave ledge. Why not change the bags over? It was true that their contents were shaped differently, but that might be fixed by putting the wrapping paper from their lunch around the plates to make them look bulkier.

The more she thought about it, the more the idea appealed to her. Wrapping the paper around the plates would protect them, and leaving the remains of their lunch in their place might even fool Hassan, provided he didn't check the bag. If they had put the bag back on the ledge in the Banqueting Hall, he might have done no more than glance up at it to make sure it was still there. Perhaps he would do the same in the Monastery.

She counted the seconds until she decided it must be safe to move. Then she got to her feet. The sudden movement woke Kevin, who opened one eye and looked at her lazily.

'Is Ali back?' he asked.

'Nuala shook her head. 'But d'you know what ...' she began.

Kevin closed the eye again.

'Tell me about it when Ali gets back,' he said, sounding absurdly like their mother.

She was about to tell him anyway, but then she remembered how long it took Kevin to wake up properly. This was no job for someone who was half-asleep, and she would have to go right now, before Ali got back. She took down the pink plastic bag with the remains of their picnic from the ledge, and went to the lip of the cave.

It was awkward getting down. She knew she ought to jump, as Ali had done, but he was much lighter than her. She sat down and reached for the stepping-stone rock, but her short legs got her nowhere near it. There was nothing for it but to put the bag down, roll over on her stomach and reach backwards for it. It was undignified but there was no-one to see. She managed to lower herself down and collect up the bag again, then she stepped down onto the wadi, took a quick look around – just in case – and raced across to the Monastery.

In the dim light inside, the building looked as empty as before. The main chamber was bare and so was the small inner room. There was nothing hidden behind the little stone altar, and no plastic bag leaned against the wall in any dark corner. Had she only dreamed she had seen Hassan? Or was it a trick of the sun, like a desert mirage, because he was so much in her thoughts? Maybe some other business had brought him to the Monastery? She felt in every little niche, hoping to find some hidden recess, and peered up at the ceiling in search of projecting ledges, but there were none.

It was childish to be so disappointed, she knew, but it had been such a good plan. She was glad now that she had said nothing to Kevin. He would only have laughed at her. She dumped her bag down on the edge of the altar, and fished out a tissue from her pocket. To her utter amazement, there was a soft clunk and the bag disappeared. She felt along the top of the altar. The flat stone which covered it didn't quite reach to the end at one side. As she groped with her hand – for it was hard to see in the dim light – she felt the stone move. As she pressed it, the stone tilted until, peering into the dark recess beneath, she could just see two pink plastic bags, sitting side by side.

She let go of the stone and it swung back to its level position. At once she pressed it again and this time, as it tilted, she reached down and lifted out the nearest bag. Opening it, she found herself staring at the remains of their picnic. Hardly daring to breathe, for the weight of the coke bottles could have smashed the egg-shell-thin Nabatean pottery if they had fallen directly on top of it, she reached in a second time. When she opened the second bag, she saw once again the dark tomato red of the plates, miraculously no more cracked and chipped than before.

Quickly, she took the big wad of paper from the first bag and wrapped it around the plates. Then she compared the two bags. They still didn't look the same, so she took one of the coke bottles out and thrust it down the side of the plates. With only the jar and two bottles, laid flat, the picnic rubbish could have been pottery. After all, once Hassan took the bag from its hiding place he would know anyway. With great care, she put the rubbish bag back under the altar slab and returned the slab to its closed position. With her heart banging against her ribs, she carried the other bag to the door of the Monastery.

No sooner had she stepped out into the heat of the wadi than she heard Ali's high-pitched call and saw him herding the goats towards the cave. Now she would have to wait until they got back to Wadi Musa to tell Kevin of her find.

It was difficult to climb into the cave with the bag, and to put it back on the ledge without the others noticing. But by watching for the right moment, while Kevin and Ali were studying some berries Ali had picked on the mountain top, she managed it. Even then, though, she couldn't relax. The goats munched away at the scrub in front of the Monastery and Kevin and Ali were fooling around, wrestling and throwing pebbles at a stone set up on a rock, but Nuala was tense, ready to seize the bag before anyone might take it up carelessly. Then, alert though she was, a new danger caught her unprepared.

'Hey!' Kevin shouted. 'Why don't we put one of the coke bottles on the rock? It would make a great target!'

Nuala struggled to her feet, ready to snatch the bag, but Ali shook his head.

'Would break,' he said.

'What harm if it does?' Kevin shrugged.

'Get money for empty bottles,' Ali explained.

Immediately Nuala felt guilty, as she collapsed back on the rugs. Her bag-swapping would cost him the price of two empty coke bottles, and maybe the screw-top jar had a value too. Then she decided that her mother and the museum would surely pay him that and more in return for the pottery. She didn't know what she would do when they got back to Umm al Biyara and Ali looked for his empties though. Perhaps by then she could risk telling him the truth, though she would feel safer waiting until they were through the Siq or with her mother.

When Ali said it was time to go, Nuala took up the bag as casually as she could manage. Then she realised she would be unable to get down from the cave with it in her hand. She put it down while she slid onto the stone in the same undignified way as before. But when she went to collect the bag she saw it in Ali's hand. She was still trying to think how she would get it back from him when she saw to her surprise that Ali was driving the goats up the wadi away from the city.

'Where are we going?' she asked.

'Goats need water,' he told her.

A short distance from the cave he turned to the left around a spur of rock. They took a track that went round the back of the cliffs behind the cave.

'This is other end of Wadi Musa,' he told them.

They were still climbing, instead of descending as Nuala had expected, so she was glad enough to have both hands free. But she kept a wary eye on the plastic bag swinging from Ali's hand, glad that he didn't want to break what he believed to be his coke bottles. Suddenly, the goat Ali had called Allat stopped and raised her head, sniffing the air. Then she gave a loud bleat. Immediately, all three goats raced on ahead towards a cleft in the rocks, from where the mountain sloped down to the wadi once more.

'Goats smell water,' Ali chuckled.

'Oh, yes, I see it,' Nuala said. A slab of concrete crossed what looked like a small stream running out from the crevice.

There was only a trickle in the dried-up stream bed. All the same, the goats pushed on across the slab to where two stone steps faced the crevice. Soon all that could be seen of them were three happily wagging tails.

'You like drink?' Ali asked.

'Is it all right to drink the water?' Nuala asked, remembering what Mr Houston had said about sticking to bottled water.

'This pure water,' Ali told her proudly. 'Come straight from mountain. Prophet Moses struck rock and out come water.'

'Moses?' Kevin echoed in surprise. 'You mean Moses from the Bible?'

'Is Moslem prophet,' Ali explained, 'but Christian prophet too, I think.'

'And you mean this is the actual rock he struck with his staff?' Nuala asked incredulously.

Ali nodded. 'Water run all way to village of Wadi Musa, but dry up fast. Wadi Musa mean Valley of Moses.'

'I wonder does Mum know that?' Nuala said.

By now the sound of the goats noisily lapping water was easing.

'I get water,' Ali told them.

Nuala saw her opportunity and tried to take the plastic bag out of his hand.

'I'll hold this while you get it,' she told him.

'I take bottle for water,' Ali argued, resisting her.

'I'll give it to you,' Nuala cried, snatching the bag from him in her desperation. Thank goodness she had kept one bottle back, she thought, as she took it from the bag and held it out to him.

Ali took the bottle and, pushing the goats aside, filled it from the bubbling spring. Then he handed it to Nuala.

'Tastes good,' he encouraged.

Nuala took a long slug from the bottle. The water was cool, clear and sweet-tasting. Kevin and Ali each drank from it too before Ali refilled it.

'Take for later,' he said, holding out his hand for the bag.

Instead, Nuala took the bottle from him and re-placed it carefully by the side of the plates.

'I'll carry this for a bit,' she said, walking on so decisively that Ali didn't bother arguing.

They were going downhill now, sometimes quite steeply. Often Nuala had to steady herself with one hand against the cliff as they crossed deep crevices or ravines. Carrying the bag made it more difficult, but she was afraid to trust it to anyone else. If Ali had opened it himself to get the bottle he would have noticed at once there were no others. Now it was filled with water, he might open the bag without warning in search of a drink, so she struggled on.

As the descent became less steep and Nuala was able to look around her, she noticed the cliffs were beginning to turn orange like they had done the previous day. Evening was approaching. Suddenly the goats quickened their step again.

'What is it this time?' Kevin asked. 'More water?'

Ali laughed.

'Know they are near home,' he said, and Nuala recognised the shape of the cliffs ahead. They had reached Umm al Biyara.

At any moment, Ali would be looking for the empties. She clutched the bag tightly, wondering what she should do, but to her relief, Ali said nothing.

'Pic-nic okay?' Ali's mother asked.

'Deadly!' Kevin nodded enthusiastically.

'Lovely, thanks – I mean *shukran*,' Nuala added hastily, feeling that Kevin might be misunderstood, but Ali's mother was relying on his expression.

When the goats were once more happily grazing by the cave, she spoke softly to Ali in Arabic. Ali nodded and turned to Kevin.

'Now we go to High Place,' he said. 'Then meet my father at Treasury. He come with truck from Bedouin tea place. Bring us through Siq.'

'Great,' Nuala said, walking off quickly lest he should notice she still held the plastic bag, but it was Kevin who mentioned it first.

'Ya eejit!' he cried suddenly. 'You forgot to give the picnic things back to Ali's mother.'

'We give my father,' Ali told him. 'Take to Wadi Musa with other empty bottles.'

'See!' Nuala said, sticking out her tongue at Kevin. 'Now who's the eejit?'

They passed the entrance to the Banqueting Hall. Kevin was for going in to see if the plates had been returned to their old hiding place, but Ali said they must hurry before the light went. Nuala had to turn her face away to hide a smile. Kevin would laugh when she told him, and Ali too, as soon as they were safely through the Siq.

'No wonder they call this the High Place,' Kevin panted twenty minutes later. 'There must be at least a thousand steps up to it!'

'Is only seven hundred feet above city,' Ali laughed. 'Monastery at Al-Deir is higher.'

'But the way up here is much steeper than any track we took today,' Nuala gasped. 'I don't think I could have done it if someone hadn't cut all these steps. I can't see many tourists coming all the way up here.'

'A few come in the morning,' Ali told her. 'Now is too late.'

Kevin stopped at the top of the last flight to get his breath back. A steep track covered in rubble lay ahead of them, with not a single step to make it easier.

'Imagine the Nabateans coming up here in a great procession,' he said, looking back down at the zig-zag of steps they had climbed. 'Winding their way up the mountain to sacrifice at the altar.'

'All dressed in white,' Nuala added. 'Led by the priest carrying a big knife and someone leading the goat for sacrificing.'

'Or a man or woman with their hands tied behind their back,' Kevin said, grinning.

'Don't be so bloodthirsty!' Nuala scolded. 'How would you like it if it was *you*?'

'Come,' said Ali. 'Mountains turn gold. Is getting late.'

'I'm not sure I can,' Nuala panted. 'That track looks awful steep.'

'Is only little way,' Ali said. 'I take bag.' And before Nuala could stop him, he had taken the plastic bag from her hand and was halfway up the track with it.

With the energy of desperation, she raced after him, Kevin following more slowly. At the top, Nuala stopped in surprise. She didn't know quite what she had expected, but it certainly wasn't what she saw. The rocky mountaintop had been levelled to form a stone terrace, from which steps led up to an altar and, beside it, a small round basin.

'For blood of sacrifice,' Ali told her.

'But what's that thing like a bath?' Kevin asked, pointing to a big rectangular stone basin nearby. 'Was that for blood too?'

'Was for sacrifice. Was dedicated to Dhu-Shara before shrine. Then put on altar for killing. Then blood run into basin.'

'And there's another of those Egyptian things,' Nuala pointed out, starting to climb a short flight of steps leading up to it.

'Obelisk,' Ali nodded, but Kevin was more interested in the sacrificial ritual.

'Mr Houston said there was a drain which carried the blood all the way down the side of the mountain,' he said, examining the basin.

'Is there,' Ali told him, pointing to where an outlet led to a culvert cut into the rock.

'Wow!' Kevin cried, peering over the edge of the stone platform, trying to see where the culvert ran. 'What a drop! I didn't realise we were quite so high! No wonder it's so cold up here. And look! There's the drain, running right around the mountain!'

On the narrow platform at the foot of the obelisk, Nuala turned to see where Kevin was pointing. As she did so, she heard the sound of a step behind her but, before she could turn around again, her arms were seized from behind in a strong grip. She cried out, struggling to free herself.

'Be still, girl!' came a harsh voice that made Nuala's blood run cold. 'If you move you fall and is very long way. I think no-one live after a such dreadful accident.'

CHAPTER SEVEN

The Second Trap

The two boys swung around when they heard Nuala's cry. For a second they were struck dumb at the sight of the tall figure of Hassan, suspended between mountain and sky beside the great obelisk. He seemed to them to have appeared by magic, like a stage demon in a puff of smoke. Then Kevin got his voice back.

'Let her go!' he yelled.

'I hold her only for safety,' Hassan replied calmly, though there was something about the way he said it that was far from reassuring. 'You want that I let her fall?'

'She won't fall if you leave her alone,' Kevin shouted. 'Just let go of her!'

But although he tried to sound tough, his words echoed back to him weakly. He turned to Ali to back him up but he, who had led them so surely all day, now stood as if paralysed, his eyes wide with fear.

'First tell me what is in bag,' Hassan ordered, without relaxing his grip on Nuala's arms.

Ali and Kevin both looked down in surprise at the pink plastic bag, still dangling from Ali's hand.

'Is only empty bottles from pic-nic,' Ali said.

'You show me,' Hassan ordered again. Kevin laughed aloud as he remembered that he too had mistaken the picnic things for the bag holding the Nabatean pottery.

'No problem,' he said. 'Show him, Ali.'

'No!' Nuala screamed. 'Why should he have to see?'

'Because you say just now you were at Al-Deir,' Hassan told her.

'I take goats for grazing,' Ali protested. 'I show you what is in bag.' He ran up the steps to the obelisk eagerly, to give Hassan no cause for annoyance with him.

'No!' Nuala screamed again.

'Don't be silly, Nuala,' Kevin said. 'It's not worth having a row over, and the joke will be on him.'

On the narrow ledge in front of the obelisk, Ali opened the bag and held it wide.

'But where are other bottles?' he cried, seeing only one.

'And what is in paper?' Hassan asked in turn, his voice now cold and hard as steel. Ali shook his head in puzzlement.

'You take off paper now,' Hassan ordered. 'Very carefully so you break nothing.'

Ali did as he was told, while Nuala struggled helplessly in Hassan's grip. When the last wrapping was removed to reveal the red and black Nabatean plates, Kevin as well as Ali cried out in amazement.

'You think you fool Hassan!'

The man's voice had lost its icy control now. Nuala could feel his whole body trembling with rage.

'They knew nothing about it,' she sobbed. 'Honestly! There was a bag exactly the same with the empties in it and I swapped them around without telling anyone.'

'So you want I punish only you?' Hassan roared.

'If you hurt her you'll be sorry,' Kevin screamed. 'Quick, Ali! Get help!'

'Stay where you are!'

There was such menace in Hassan's voice that Ali stood rooted to the spot in terror.

'If you want that this girl live you do as I say, or ...'

Still holding Nuala pinioned by the arms, he pushed her closer to the cliff edge. She could see the mountainside falling steeply below her. With a harsh cry, a hawk far below swooped on some tiny helpless creature sheltering in the scrub beneath. Too terrified even to scream, Nuala felt herself raised up as the hawk and the wadi seemed to change places with the sky. Her stomach heaved and she felt a terrible hammering in her head.

'I'll do it! I'll do it!' Kevin yelled desperately. 'Just let her go and I'll do whatever you say!'

'See that you do,' Hassan said coldly, setting Nuala back down at the base of the obelisk. Her legs seemed to have turned to jelly and she collapsed in a heap against the pediment.

Hassan left her there. He plunged a hand in amongst his white robes and it came out again holding a small black automatic.

'I tell you he have gun!' Ali sobbed.

Hassan smiled, but it was not a pleasant smile. 'You talk too much, Ali, and now you help strangers against Bedouin. You do as I tell you or you in bad trouble.'

'I do it! I do it!' Ali wailed, his eyes rolling in terror.

'Then you put treasure in bag, very carefully, and lay behind obelisk.'

Revolver in hand, Hassan kept a wary eye on all three of them, but Ali could not wait to show his willingness to obey. Nuala was beyond moving and Kevin was too afraid for her even to think of escape. As soon as he was satisfied that the treasure was safely hidden, Hassan called to Kevin.

'Come,' he ordered and, as Kevin joined Ali at the top of the steps, 'you carry girl down.'

'I can walk,' Nuala protested weakly but, if Kevin

and Ali hadn't been supporting her on either side she would have fallen. Hassan followed them, the revolver still in his hand. When they came to the rectangular basin which Ali had said once held sacrificial victims, Hassan gestured towards it.

'Get in,' he ordered.

'In *there*?' Kevin asked in horror.

'Do as I say,' Hassan thundered, 'or …'

He left his sentence unfinished but Kevin hesitated no longer and all three of them climbed obediently into the stone basin.

'Lie down on face,' came the next order and this time there were no questions.

'Now,' he said, as he tied their hands together behind their backs with something that felt like twine, 'A man come here soon. If you speak, make small sound even, I shoot.'

Packed tightly side-by-side like sardines and tied together like a chain gang, the three of them lay face downwards on the hard stone floor, hardly daring to breathe. After a while, they heard the sound of feet on the rubble path below, and the panting of a climber out of condition. Then they heard a voice that Kevin and Nuala both recognised.

'*Mein Gott!*' it exclaimed. 'Vy must ve meet in such a place?'

'Because here no-one comes.'

Hassan's voice came from very close. Nuala thought he must be sitting on the edge of the stone basin, so that he would be between the newcomer and themselves. The basin was so deep, though, that someone would have to look right over the top of it to see them, lying at the bottom. She felt the sickness in her stomach rising and became terrified she might be sick.

'Also,' Hassan continued pointedly, 'is on top of mountain. Make better bargain on edge of precipice.'

'*Gott in Himmel!*' the German cried shrilly. 'Are you making a threat?'

'I ask only for fair price.'

'I have been in touch with my embassy and now can increase the price to one thousand Deutsche Marks.'

'That is good. You have money with you?'

'But you have told me you must make a journey to get the treasure. I will pay nothing until I see what you have.'

'No journey. I get treasure. You wait here.'

Nuala could hear Hassan's footsteps moving away. He must be climbing the steps to the obelisk, to fetch the plastic bag that Ali had hidden. All she had achieved by her clever plan had been to save Hassan a journey to Al-Deir to fetch the pottery, now he had managed to up the price.

Could she attract the German's attention while

Hassan was up at the obelisk, or could he shoot them from there? Even if she could, would the German help them? He would hardly be a match for Hassan with his gun, and anyway he might not be anxious to help witnesses to his smuggling arrangements. Before she could decide, Hassan's voice interrupted her thoughts.

'You pay me now,' he said.

'First you must show me vat you have.'

Nuala heard the rustling of the bag opening.

'One, two, three.' It was Hassan's voice again. 'Like before.'

'*Ach, jah! Das ist wunderbar!* So I vill give you this and you vill count, please.'

Nuala could hear Hassan muttering to himself in Arabic as he flicked his way through the banknotes. Finally he must have been satisfied for, when he next spoke, his voice sounded triumphant.

'Now go. Take to embassy. I wait little time, so not seen with you. You come back three-four months. Maybe I have more.'

'Then I will say "*auf wiedersehen*"!'

There was a scrabbling on the path and the sound of the German swearing under his breath as he slid on the rubble going down. Surely Hassan would release them now? But there was only a long silence. Could he have gone and left them? What seemed like hours passed. Nuala was just plucking up courage to say something to Kevin when she heard Hassan's voice once more.

'Now I have problem only with you.'

'Untie us,' Kevin said boldly, his voice echoing strangely inside the stone basin, 'and your problem is solved.'

'You know I cannot do this,' Hassan answered. 'Then you tell everything.'

'No, we won't!' Kevin cried. 'I promise you! Let us go now and we'll say nothing to anybody!'

'This promise you would not keep. Now you have heard all. Is not possible I let you go.'

'But you can't keep us prisoners for ever!' Nuala gasped.

'Don't you understand?' Kevin cried. 'He means to kill us!'

Ali spoke then for the first time, crying out in a flood of Arabic. The words came tumbling over each other in his urgency and Nuala could only guess that he was pleading for his life. Hassan's short, gruff reply needed no translation.

'You can't shoot us!' Nuala cried. 'Lots of people knew we were coming here. They'll be looking for us. If they find we're dead they'll catch you and hang you!'

'You think Hassan stupid?' The voice was angry

again. 'I do not shoot. You will have accident. Last year tourist fall from High Place. You die same way.'

'All three of us?' Kevin shouted. 'Who's going to believe that?'

'They believe.' Hassan was calm now, sure of himself. 'One slip, others try to catch. All fall.'

'With our hands tied?'

It was Kevin again, his mind working overtime.

'You think you trick Hassan, but I untie one by one. You die first.'

He grabbed Kevin's left arm, jerking it up so that Kevin cried out.

'No!' Nuala screamed, as she heard the click of a flick-knife opening, and she knew Hassan was bending over the basin.

Suddenly the sound of voices drifted up to them on the still evening air.

'Someone's coming!' Kevin shouted. 'Now you'll have to let us go!'

Nuala was straining her ears for more hopeful sounds. She heard Hassan run to the edge of the platform, but he returned at once.

'No-one comes,' he said. 'Is only Bedouin family coming from Siq to Al-Numair.'

Nuala started to sob.

'Perhaps others come this way,' Hassan continued. 'Is time now. Is better no-one near when I make accident. Soon will be dark, then no-one come. Now I put money in safe place. After dark is dangerous taking much money through Siq.'

Then, for the first time, Nuala heard Hassan laugh, but it was not a pleasant sound.

'You will wait for me, I think. So, *Sa'alem!* Then the sound of his feet sliding over the rubble on the path below told them that he had begun his descent.

'What are we going to do?' she asked despairingly, as soon as she thought he would be out of earshot.

'Can do nothing,' Ali wailed. 'Is your fault. I tell you Hassan bad. Why you not listen Ali!'

'The maddening thing is that I've got my scout knife in my pocket,' Kevin said, 'if only I could get at it.'

'Maybe you can,' Nuala said, hope coming back into her voice.

'With my hands tied behind my back and strung up to you?' Kevin asked bitterly. 'If Hassan had only cut me free before he heard the voices, I could have managed it.'

'He'd only have tied you up again before he left,' Nuala pointed out, 'but the knife's worth a try. Anything's better than lying here waiting to die like sacrifices to Dhu-Shara. Which pocket is your knife in?'

'The right one.'

'That's a good start!'

'What's good about it?'

'It's the outside pocket. You'd never manage to get at the one I'm lying up against. Maybe if we all move our arms as far as we can to the right at the same time you might be able to get it.'

'We can have a go,' Kevin agreed. 'D'you understand, Ali? I'll count to three and on three we all reach our hands as far to the right as we can manage. Are you ready? One, two, *three*!'

They all strained but, after much grunting and wriggling, Kevin had to admit defeat.

'I almost made it,' he panted, 'but you were dragging me back all the time and my wrists are throbbing like mad.'

'I know why,' Nuala told him.

'Of course,' Kevin snapped. 'The twine's cutting into them.'

'I don't mean that,' Nuala said, exasperated. 'I mean, I know why you couldn't reach your pocket. Ali and I put our arms as far over as we could but we didn't bend them. If Ali and I tried to reach our own pockets too it would bring the twine up further. Let's try again. Okay, Ali?'

'Ali have no pocket,' he replied in a sad, hopeless tone.

Nuala stifled her impatience. After all, it was her fault that they were in this mess.

'That doesn't matter, Ali,' she said gently. 'Just try

to put your hand where your right pocket would be if you had one. Are you ready?'

'Ready,' Kevin answered. 'One, two, *three*!'

They all strained again until their arms and shoulders ached.

'I nearly had it that time!' Kevin gasped. 'I could feel the tip of the handle against my middle finger. Try and give me another inch or two.'

They all twisted as far as the twine would allow, struggling till the sweat broke out on their foreheads.

'A bit more!' Kevin panted.

'I can't!' Nuala gasped. 'My arms are being dragged out of me as it is!'

She was almost lying on top of Kevin and Ali's light little body was pushing against her left hip and shoulder. Suddenly, Kevin gave a shout of triumph and the tugging on her wrist eased.

'I've got it!' he yelled. 'I've got it!'

'Allah be praised!' Ali cried.

'Can you open it?' Nuala asked anxiously. 'It would be easier if it was a flick knife like Hassan has.'

'Will you stay quiet!' Kevin snapped. 'Each time you move I nearly drop it.'

For what seemed an age he wriggled his shoulders and arched his back, struggling to open the knife despite the cord binding his wrists. Suddenly Nuala felt his body relax.

'Now,' he breathed, 'all I have to do is cut us free.'

He soon found, however, that that was a great deal easier said than done.

'You'll both have to reach to the right again,' he said, 'only this time I'll be turning the opposite way, so our hands meet. Are you ready? One, two, *three*!'

A yelp from Nuala told him that her hands had come in contact with the open knife.

'Will you go easy with that knife?' she yelled. 'It's sharp!'

'Sorry,' Kevin told her, 'but it's difficult when I can't see what I'm doing.'

He felt with the other hand for her wrist and found the cord.

'I'll try not to hurt you,' he said, 'but a cut hand's a lot better than being thrown from the side of a mountain.'

'Just don't cut it off altogether,' Nuala said. She gritted her teeth against the pain, as Kevin began sawing at the twine. Working behind his back with the knife gripped at a strange angle, he seemed to be getting nowhere for a while. Then one of the strands snapped. Panting with the effort, he kept on sawing away. Then, with the weight of the two bodies straining on them, the other strands gave way one by one, and Kevin rolled clear from Nuala, the knife still in his hand.

Rubbing her sore and reddened wrists, Nuala struggled to a sitting position. She felt something wet on her bare ankle and saw blood dripping from a cut on the back of her left hand. Licking the cut to try to stop the bleeding, she began to fumble with the knot that bound Kevin's hands, but the twine had bitten too deeply into his wrist.

'Don't waste time,' Kevin shouted. 'Hassan may come back at any minute.'

'I've got pins and needles in my hand,' Nuala explained apologetically, as she took the knife clumsily from him and began to try to cut through the twine, made slippery from her own blood.

'For heaven's sake!' Kevin roared impatiently. 'If I could cut you loose with my hands tied behind my back surely to goodness you can manage with a few pins and needles!'

'Keep still, will you?' Nuala begged. 'I'm doing my best.'

Even though she could see what she was doing, it was difficult to cut the cord without cutting Kevin. But in the end she managed it and Kevin, grabbing the knife from her, quickly did the same for Ali.

'Is hand hurting?' Ali asked, as he saw the blood stains on Nuala's white T-shirt, but Kevin had no time to waste on sympathy.

'Is there another way down from here?' he asked Ali.

Ali shook his head. 'Is too dangerous,' he replied.

'Then we must get down fast and out of sight before Hassan comes back,' Kevin said tensely. 'Hurry, can't you.'

Nuala had listened to both Hassan and the German slipping on the rubble path, but it was not until she had to negotiate it herself in the dark that she realised how dangerous it was. She heard Kevin curse as a stone rolled from beneath his feet. He recovered his balance with difficulty. Then Ali cried out a warning, just as her own feet went from under her. She might have met the fate Hassan had planned for them if Ali hadn't grabbed hold of her.

'Hurry no good if fall,' he pointed out.

'I can't seem to balance properly,' she said, shame-faced.

'You have shock,' he said, 'so must go slow.'

It was strange, Nuala thought, how Ali had seemed so much the weakest of them when Hassan had been there. Now they were free, even though danger still threatened, he had once again become their guide and leader.

Once they reached the steps they were able to move faster. They could even take two steps at a time at the bottom of each flight, when there was a flat space on the bend to jump onto. Each time she landed, Nuala peered through the darkness below for signs of Hassan returning. On the steps themselves though, she didn't dare raise her eyes in case she stumbled again. Finally, they reached the wadi and they all breathed a big sigh of relief.

'I don't feel quite so afraid of Hassan down here,' she gasped.

'You forget he have gun,' Ali argued. 'We must hide in cave until he pass.'

'No time,' Kevin panted. 'We must tell someone about the treasure, so the police can catch that German.'

'Life more important than treasure!' Ali protested. But he kept going and, though Kevin and Nuala were out of breath and slowing, his thin wiry body seemed tireless.

'Wadi Musa,' he called out a few minutes later, pointing ahead, and they saw, beyond the blackness of a projecting cliff on the right, the main tourist route from the Siq into Petra.

'Oh, thank goodness,' Nuala panted.

It was at that moment that they heard a voice. 'Is further than by desert highway, but tourists like very much. You see Crusader fortress at Kerak and mosaic map of Palestine at Madaba.'

'Is my father!' Ali cried joyfully.

Then they heard another voice, and this time all three recognised it. 'So, I vill take this route. *Danke sehr.*'

'The German!' Kevin gasped and, with one accord, they summoned up fresh energy and ran out into Wadi Musa. There they saw, by the light of his headlamps, Ali's father loading a crate of Coke from his truck into the boot of a grey Audi. At that moment, the car engine started and they saw the German at the wheel.

At the sound of running feet behind him, Ali's father turned, one hand suspended in the act of closing the car boot. On a sudden impulse, Kevin pushed him aside and jumped into the boot beside the crate. The lid of the boot fell shut. Hearing the slam, the German drove off at speed. He slackened only slightly as the beam of his lights swept across the Treasury, and then swung left to disappear into the depths of the Siq. Ali's father stood staring after the car, his mouth open.

'Quick!' Nuala yelled. 'We must stop him!' And she ran towards the truck.

Ali let out one of his floods of Arabic. Whatever he said caused his father to leap into the driving seat of the truck and start up the engine. Ali and Nuala scrambled into the passenger seat.

'Why your brother do this crazy thing?' Ali's father asked Nuala, as the truck began to gather speed.

'I suppose he thinks the treasure's in the car,' Nuala told him, 'but he must be completely mad!'

Kevin had just begun to think the same thing. His one idea had been to get into the car without being seen by the driver and, for a while, he had been delighted with the success of his action. In any case, he was completely exhausted and, even curled up uncomfortably beside the crate, he had been happy just to be lying down. Only after he had been flung roughly against the side of the boot as the car turned into the Siq did he realise just how uncomfortable a journey lay ahead of him.

He began to devise a plan. The German would never drive all the way to Amman without stopping. As soon as he stopped, Kevin thought, he would try to grab the pink plastic bag and get away. If he couldn't manage that, he would puncture the tyres with his scout's knife. Then at least the German couldn't take it to the embassy. He could feel the throbbing of the car engine, so he would know the minute it was switched off. He wouldn't be able to see when the German had left the car, so he would have to raise the boot very cautiously, inch by inch, and peer out without attracting attention.

It was then that it struck him. The boot would have locked when it slammed shut, and there was no way he could open it from the inside. He had escaped from Hassan only to fall into a trap of his own making.

CHAPTER EIGHT

The Chase over the Mountains

As the truck swung into the Siq, Ali's father said something in Arabic and Ali turned to Nuala.

'What Kevin think is true,' he told her. 'My father say he see pink plastic bag same like this one on back seat of car.'

Then Nuala noticed that there was yet another of the pink plastic bags lying on a little shelf under the bonnet. She had been right. Everyone in Petra used them for everything.

Her thoughts were suddenly interrupted when Ali seized her arm and pointed ahead of them with a trembling hand. Peering through the windscreen to find out what was causing him such alarm, Nuala saw the figure of a man, caught in the beam of the truck headlamps. Even though they were with Ali's father, she too felt a shiver of fear, for there was no mistaking the hawk-like nose of Hassan. Then, as he raised one hand to shield his eyes, she realised he was blinded by the lights.

'It's all right,' she said to Ali. 'He can't see us.'

'You have trouble with Hassan?' his father asked a little anxiously, as they drove past.

'I tell you other time,' Ali said. 'Now most important we catch car.'

'We've got to overtake it and make it stop,' Nuala explained, 'because Kevin won't be able to let himself out of the boot. If the German doesn't open it for a few days he could starve to death.'

'He open to take out crate,' Ali's father said, 'and now is cool, but when sun come up will be very hot. With no air in boot will be bad for him.'

'Then we must catch him soon,' Nuala cried. 'Please try to go faster!'

'Not possible in Siq. Later we go faster.'

'But not as fast as a big car like that!' Nuala muttered, worried.

'This very fast truck,' Ali said proudly, 'and all bottles now empty so truck light.'

'I give last full crate to German,' his father agreed, as he slowed for the sharp right turn at the far end of the Siq. 'He pay me for bottles and crate too.'

'All the same,' Nuala persisted, 'he's got a good start on us.'

'My father know road better than German,' Ali

assured her. 'You soon see how fast we go.'

And so she did, for Ali's father accelerated so violently on the rough sandy track when they came out of the Siq that she was flung heavily against the back of her seat. Instinctively clutching at the shelf in front of her, she realised that her hand was still bleeding. She shoved it into her mouth and then wrapped it inside her T-shirt. The T-shirt was already covered in blood anyway, and the inside would be cleaner than the outside. Her hand was quite sore, but she had forgotten all about it in the panic of their escape, and she soon forgot about it again.

'I don't see any sign of the car,' she worried, gazing through the windscreen at the empty wadi in the beam of the truck's headlamps.

'I know which way he go,' Ali's father reassured her. 'He go by King's Highway. In daylight tourists sometimes take this route but at night he see nothing and is very long journey – maybe five, six hours.'

'Oh no!' Nuala cried. 'It will be awful for Kevin unless we can catch him.'

They were tearing through the village of Wadi Musa now, the engine roaring as they climbed the steep hill past their house. But, instead of taking the road through Ma'an on to the desert highway, the truck swung left on to the even steeper track leading up into the mountains towards Shaubak.

'No-one drive on King's Highway at night,' Ali's father explained, as he changed into first gear. 'If German have trouble with car is no-one to help him. Only crazy man go that way at night when is only three hours by desert highway and also patrols for helping motorist.'

'But that's why he's going the other way,' Nuala shouted. 'Don't you see? He doesn't want to risk being stopped by a patrol when he has the treasure in the car!'

'Maybe other thing stop him,' Ali's father said ominously, as the truck followed the curve of the mountain road. Nuala could see the lights of Wadi Musa behind them far, far below. 'This road has many bends. At night is dangerous. Not for me. I know road well. For stranger is different. He go too fast he drive off cliff.'

'Then we must overtake him before he has time to do anything dangerous,' Nuala urged.

'Overtaking not possible,' Ali's father said. 'Is too narrow.'

'Oh no!' Nuala said again. 'I do hope Kevin's all right.'

As it happened, Kevin was feeling less and less all right with every kilometre. He was being flung about first one way and then another as the car swung violently around bend after bend. Right turns were the worst, because then he fell against the crate and its sharp corners, and metal-capped bottles stuck into him until he was bruised all over. He had begun to feel sick too, for, whenever the car was being driven uphill in low gear, some of the fumes from the exhaust seemed to be finding their way into the boot.

He had no idea where they were. He only knew from what he had overheard that they weren't going by the desert highway and, indeed, his senses told him that the route was very different from the broad, flat, dusty main road to the capital.

He decided he would have to get some air soon, even if it meant giving himself up. He began to shout and hammer on the inside of the boot in an effort to attract the German's attention, but the car didn't even slow. Probably the German couldn't hear him over the noise of the engine and the grit that kept rattling on the underside of the mudguards. Kevin's efforts left him gasping for breath and he soon gave up the attempt. He would have to wait until the car stopped and there was silence. What he would do when he got out he didn't know. His plans had all relied on the German not knowing he was there, but now he would be forced to seek his help.

He wondered what sort of man the German was.

It was hard to tell from his two conversations with Hassan. If Hassan had been driving, Kevin thought, he would rather take his chances in the boot than throw himself on his tender mercies, but surely no-one working in an embassy would go in for murder? On the other hand, being caught smuggling Nabatean pottery would probably carry a long sentence and people did desperate things to stay out of gaol, especially if there was no-one around to see.

It struck Kevin that they hadn't passed a single car since they left Petra. He was sure if they had he would have heard it. It might be wiser to try to hang on until they reached Amman, so that he could get out where there would be plenty of witnesses. All the same, he hoped they'd get there soon, because it was becoming more and more smelly in the boot. He decided to think of something else to take his mind off his discomfort.

He began to wonder what the others had thought when they saw him hide in the boot. Had Ali's father taken Nuala home and had she told their mother what had happened? He hoped she wouldn't be angry or worried, but he knew she would probably be both. He wondered what she was saying about him and whether Mr Houston would ring the German Embassy ...

Nuala gasped as the headlights swept the ravine far below, and the truck swayed for a moment as it swung left and downwards on to a narrow bridge spanning the chasm. She clutched Ali's arm as the brakes screamed and the gears made a grinding noise. Then they were roaring up the mountain track on the far side and swinging right once more.

'Whoever built this crazy road?' she gasped.

'Was built for camels, not cars,' Ali's father grinned. 'Was part of old trade route from Egypt to Damascus.'

'We learn this in school,' Ali added. 'Rich caravans took silks and spices and precious stones for selling. Nabateans robbed merchants and hid stolen riches in Petra. Later, merchants pay Nabateans for safe journey.'

'A protection racket!' Nuala cried. 'I didn't think they went in for them in those days.'

Then they rounded another bend in the mountain and Ali gave a shout. Far ahead of them were two pinpricks of red.

'Is it the German's car?' Nuala asked eagerly.

'Now we gain on him,' Ali's father said, nodding.

'But how will we make him stop if we can't overtake him?' Nuala worried.

'First we catch him. Then we make him stop.'

'But if he sees us behind him, won't he only go faster?' Nuala persisted.

'Why he do this? Not know we come after him.'

'With treasure he nervous all time,' Ali told his father.

He was echoing Nuala's own thoughts and she shivered. There was still the danger that their pursuit might cause the German to drive recklessly and end up in the ravine, with Kevin still locked in the boot. Were they wrong to be chasing him? But what else could they do? She tried to imagine what it must be like for Kevin, imprisoned behind those tiny pinpricks of light.

Kevin was beginning to feel drowsy. The smell from the exhaust was getting worse, but he didn't really care any more. The ache of his bruises and the cramp in his legs from the strange way he was lying had eased. He had even stopped worrying about how he was going to get out of the boot. He was dreaming that he was tucked up snug and warm in a bunk on board ship, like the time he had been with the scouts on a trip to Normandy on the Rosslare ferry. The ship was pitching and rolling, but he didn't mind because he knew that when he woke he would be in another land and it would all be strange and new and exciting.

Suddenly the boat stopped with a shudder. Had they hit a rock? Something must have gone wrong, because there was cold air flooding into the cabin as if a porthole had been blown in. Out of nowhere, the captain appeared beside his bunk and was standing looking down at him. He seemed to be surprised about something.

'*Mein Gott!*' the captain cried.

To Kevin's annoyance, he began to shake him. Kevin wished he would stop.

'You must vake up!' he kept saying.

Kevin didn't want to have to get out of his nice warm bunk. Still, he knew from the worried tone of the captain's voice that it must be an emergency. Maybe they were shipwrecked and they were abandoning ship. He would have to go up on deck and take to the lifeboat. Reluctantly he stirred and the pain came flooding back. Then he realised he was lying in a very strange position, looking up at the night sky. A man was bending over him, but he wasn't wearing a captain's uniform.

'*Gott Sie Dank!*' the man exclaimed. 'He is not dead!'

The man picked Kevin up in his arms and he felt the night air all round him. He was stiff and dizzy. Then he was sitting on the front seat of a car, having his face sponged. He licked his lips and tasted coke. This madman was washing his face in Coca-Cola! He had another lick. This time the man noticed and held the bottle to his lips. Kevin took a mouthful of coke, and then another.

'So now you are better,' the man said.

He had a foreign accent and suddenly Kevin remembered where he was and why. He tried to wriggle away from the man, but he was too weak. Anyway, it didn't look like the man was going to kill him.

'What happened?' he mumbled stupidly.

'You ask *me* this?' the German exclaimed and he sounded indignant. 'I am driving a long vay, so I must stop to make pee-pee. Then I open the boot to get a drink and find you. So now I am asking *you* vat happened. How do you get in the boot of my car?'

Kevin still felt confused, but it was clear that the man was puzzled and irritated, rather than angry. Then it struck Kevin that, although he had seen the German in the Banqueting Hall with Hassan, the German had never seen him. Nor had he known that there were three terrified young people listening to every word that passed between him and Hassan at the High Place. He had no reason to suspect that Kevin knew what was in the pink plastic bag. All Kevin had to do now was to invent some story, any story, that would explain how he had ended up in the boot. He felt sure that if only his head didn't ache so badly he might be able to think of one.

'So you are still too veak for talking,' the German

said, not unkindly. 'You tell me as ve drive, because now I am in a very great hurry.'

He shut the passenger door and went round to the driver's seat. As he did so, Kevin made a huge effort to turn his head, and glanced into the back of the car. The pink plastic bag was still there, casually lying on the seat. He felt a wave of relief. The German was not about to injure him and the treasure was still within sight. After he had rested a while, he would be able to work out a plan.

The German was fastening his seat belt. 'To take you back to Petra vould be for me impossible. At the embassy, I vill ring your parents and tell them you are safe. In the morning, someone vill take you to the jet bus to go vith the tourists to Petra.'

He was just putting his key into the ignition when they heard a truck roaring up from behind them. Hurriedly, the German re-started the engine.

'There is, I think, just room here for passing, but if I permit this ve must drive all the vay to Kerak behind this noisy truck,' he explained.

Slipping into gear, he released the handbrake, flashed his indicator and began to slide forward.

To his amazement, the truck driver responded with a high-pitched blast of his horn and increased speed.

'*Mein Gott*, vat a vay to drive on such a road!' the German cried.

Resignedly he braked, waiting for the truck to go by and, as it did, Kevin saw Ali's head framed in the near window. He opened his mouth to call out to him, but the only sound that came out was a hoarse croak and, by then, the truck had passed. Then it slewed across the road, completely blocking it, and pulled up with a scream of brakes.

'*Gott in Himmel!*' gasped the German. 'Vat does this madman think he is doing?' and he jumped from his car and ran towards the truck, shaking his fist.

'You are fortunate you do not kill someone!' he screamed as the driver opened the door of the truck.

Then he recognised the Bedouin from whom he had bought the crate of Coca-Cola.

'Vat is this?' he demanded. 'I pay you already!'

In the meantime, Ali scrambled to the ground on the far side of the truck and ran across to the Audi.

'Kevin okay!' he called joyfully to Nuala when he found Kevin, still slumped in the passenger seat.

Reassured about this, Nuala's mind focused once more on the reason for Kevin's plight. On impulse, she grabbed the pink plastic bag from the truck's bonnet. Her great plan had failed the first time but it might be worth trying again. While the German argued with Ali's father and Ali talked to Kevin, she wrenched at the handle of the rear door of the car. It was locked.

'Quick, Ali!' she said. 'Open this door!'

Ali looked at her, bewildered, but Kevin, weak though he was, found the energy to reach back with one hand and snap off the lock.

'Brill!' he whispered, as Nuala quickly slipped the bag in her hand on to the back seat and ran with the other bag to the truck. She was only just in time, for she had barely reached it when the German returned to his car.

'So,' he said to Kevin. 'I should be angry that you play this foolish trick, but you have been punished enough, I think. So now you will get out please so that I may continue my journey.'

'Thank you,' Kevin said meekly, hiding a big grin. 'I'm sorry for delaying you.'

Then, with Ali's help, he got awkwardly from the car and walked across to the truck.

'I pull over. Then you pass,' Ali's father called to the German. 'I must turn here. Or I must go all way to Kerak before I find place for turning.'

'That is vy I stop here,' the German called back. 'I vould stop sooner if I find a place to pull off the road.'

Nuala saw him glance into the back of the car before starting the engine. The pink plastic bag lay there, apparently undisturbed. As soon as the truck had straightened out, he edged past it, then he accelerated and was gone.

'I say nothing about treasure,' Ali's father told them, as they watched the tail lights of the Audi disappear around a curve in the mountainside. 'I know you will be sad, but is more important we take Kevin back safe.'

'I'm not sad at all,' Nuala laughed. 'Look!'

She took the pink plastic bag from under the bonnet and held it out to him, open wide. When he saw the plates, he gave a shout of dismay.

'But where is my tool kit?' he demanded. 'My big and little spanners and screwdriver! They cost me much money!'

'I'm sorry I had to take them,' Nuala told him, 'but I couldn't think of any other way of getting back the treasure. I'm sure my mother will buy you more. I'll ask her as soon as we get home.'

But she almost forgot in the fuss that greeted their return. She had been too worried about Kevin and the treasure to realise how late it was, and how worried their mother must have become. As they drove down the hill into Wadi Musa, she could see light streaming from their house, and a crowd of people out in the street. Amongst them were her mother, Mr Houston and a man in uniform. The minute she saw them, her mother began to shout and they had a great deal of explaining to do to calm her down.

'D'you realise we were about to send out a search

party?' her mother yelled, and the man in uniform seemed very annoyed too.

He became really excited, however, when he saw the Nabatean pottery. Then Nuala and Kevin had to convince him that they weren't trying to smuggle it out of Petra themselves. After they had told him the whole story he became a little more friendly, but by then their mother was almost hysterical, between the sight of Nuala's blood-stained T-shirt and the idea of Hassan planning to throw them from the High Place. Ali's father also became very excited, for he hadn't heard this part of the story before either, and he shouted in Arabic at the man in uniform, who questioned Ali in the same language.

'He think Hassan only threaten to frighten us,' Ali translated, 'but I tell him about man Hassan kill and about gun and he say him very bad man.'

To Nuala's surprise, however, he seemed more interested in the possibility of arresting the German than in taking any action against Hassan, and kept asking questions about the former.

'I don't think I'd know him if I saw him again,' Kevin told him. 'Except for a few seconds when it was already dark, I was in the boot all the time.'

Nuala opened her mouth to say she'd know him anywhere, but Kevin gave her a kick. Surprised, she shut her mouth.

'Why did you kick me?' she asked indignantly, after the man in uniform had gone.

'I don't want the German nicked,' Kevin said. 'He was kind to me and I don't think he's one of the higher-ups in the embassy. He could be just a go-between. Hassan is the real crook, but of course the police would much rather put all the blame on a foreigner. He even tried to blame us! It's Hassan I want to see punished.'

'He sounds an absolute monster,' Mr Houston agreed. 'But I'm not sure the German crowd should be allowed to go scot-free either. After all, if there was no market for stolen goods there'd be no thieves.'

'But he may have saved Kevin's life,' his mother said, 'and this other creature was prepared to kill him and Nuala too.'

'Also he try to kill my son,' Ali's father added. 'That German good customer of Bedouin. Buy plenty souvenirs and drinks.'

'Okay, okay,' Mr Houston laughed. 'I see I'm outvoted. Anyway, the main thing is that everyone is safe and the pottery too. Just look at it!'

And they all admired the beautiful eggshell-thin black and red plates again. Then Nuala remembered Ali's father's tool-kit.

'And he lost money he would have collected on the empties I left in the bag up at the monastery as well,' she added.

Everyone laughed at that, though Nuala couldn't see why, and Mr Houston took a handful of dollars from his pocket.

'That should cover it,' he said, handing them to Ali's father, 'and if the museum is willing to make a reward for the pottery, I'll see you're not forgotten.'

'*Shukran*,' Ali's father said, pocketing the money quickly, 'and if Kevin and Nuala want drink in Petra there will be no charge at Bedouin tea place.'

'Deadly!' Kevin cried and Nuala added: 'Thanks a lot – I mean, *shukran!*

'If the museum comes across, they should be well able to afford a few cokes,' Mr Houston told him and Kevin's eyes lit up.

'D'you think there would be enough to pay for a trip to the Gulf of Aqaba?' he asked. 'Petra is great, but you can't swim in it.'

'I'd say there would be enough for several trips,' Mr Houston told him, 'but you won't have to wait that long. I'll drive you over there myself at the weekend. Even an archaeologist is entitled to some time off, and I wouldn't mind a swim myself. I can promise you, you'll never swim in warmer water. We'll all go.'

'But I can't swim!' said a subdued voice, and for the first time Nuala became aware of Amanda, standing unnoticed on the edge of the group. It wasn't at all like Amanda, she thought, not to be at the centre of things.

Kevin felt tempted to say something cutting, but he was feeling too lazy and even slightly generous.

'I'll teach you how to swim if you'll teach me to ride,' he said. 'After all, we've got the whole summer ahead of us ...'

Other books from
The O'Brien Press

AMELIA
Siobhán Parkinson

Almost thirteen, Amelia Pim, daughter of a wealthy Dublin
Quaker family, loves frocks and parties – but now she must
learn to live with poverty and the disgrace of a mother arrested
for suffragette activities.

Paperback £3.99

NO PEACE FOR AMELIA
Siobhán Parkinson

Amelia's friend, Frederick, enlists for the Great War, whilst
servant Mary Ann's brother is involved with the Easter Rising
and wants her to hide him in the Pim home. The issues for
Amelia are love and war.

Paperback £4.50

THE CHIEFTAIN'S DAUGHTER
Sam McBratney

A boy fostered with a remote Irish tribe 1500 years ago becomes
involved in a local feud and with the fate of his beloved Frann,
the Chieftain's Daughter.

Paperback £3.99

UNDER THE HAWTHORN TREE
Marita Conlon-McKenna

Eily, Michael and Peggy are left without parents when the Great
Famine strikes. They set out on a long and dangerous journey
to find the great-aunts their mother told them about in her
stories.

Paperback £3.95

WILDFLOWER GIRL
Marita Conlon-McKenna

Peggy, from *Under the Hawthorn Tree*, is now thirteen and must leave Ireland for America. After a terrible journey on board ship, she arrives in Boston. What kind of life will she find there?

Hardback £6.95 Paperback £4.50

THE BLUE HORSE
Marita Conlon-McKenna

When their caravan burns down, Katie's family must move to live in a house on a new estate. But for Katie, this means trouble. Is she strong enough to deal with the new situation?

Paperback £3.99

THE HUNTER'S MOON
Orla Melling

Cousins Findabhair and Gwen defy an ancient law at Tara, and Findabhair is abducted. In a sequence of amazing happenings, Gwen tries to retrieve her cousin from the Otherworld.

Paperback £3.99

THE SINGING STONE
Orla Melling

A gift of ancient books sparks off a visit to Ireland by a young girl. Her destiny becomes clear – *she* has been chosen to recover the four treasures of the Tuatha de Danann. All her ingenuity and courage are needed.

Paperback £3.99

THE DRUID'S TUNE
Orla Melling

In the adventure of their lives, two teenage visitors to Ireland are hurled into the ancient past and become involved in the wild and heroic life of Cuchulainn and in the fierce battle of the Táin.

Paperback £4.50

MOONLIGHT
Michael Carroll

The body of a 10,000 year-old horse is discovered and a genetic engineer and a ruthless businessman dream of the fastest racehorse ever. But can Cathy outwit them and protect the new-born Foal?

Paperback £3.99

BIKE HUNT

Hugh Galt

Niall Quinn's new bike is stolen and he is determined to find it. Helped by the skill of Katie, and by his friend Paudge, Niall becomes entangled in a dangerous and thrilling situation in the Wicklow Mountains.

Paperback £3.95

And many more – send for our full-colour catalogue

ORDER FORM

These books are available from your local bookseller. In case of difficulty order direct from THE O'BRIEN PRESS

Please send me the books as marked

I enclose cheque / postal order for £......... (+ 50p P&P per title)

OR please charge my credit card ☐ Access / Mastercard ☐ Visa

Card number ☐☐☐☐ ☐☐☐☐ ☐☐☐☐ ☐☐☐☐

EXPIRY DATE ☐ ☐ ☐ ☐

Name: ....Tel: ....

Address: ....

....

Please send orders to : THE O'BRIEN PRESS, 20 Victoria Road, Dublin 6.
Tel: (Dublin) 4923333 Fax: (Dublin) 4922777